The Dream Traveler

The Dream Traveler

All Rights Reserved ©2013 by Daniel Gamboa
ISBN 9781490426655

For Darlene and the kids.

The Dream Traveler

4

Dear reader,

    The following story was written from the middle outward. The concept was derived from an idea of time-travel, where nothing could ever be done to change the past. And once the future was seen it became inevitable. The events were put together to tie into each other logically and with purpose. Please take your time to take notice of the small details and don't despair for any loose end, for they will be addressed as the story progresses. Enjoy.

Daniel Gamboa

Chapter 1

March, 1976.
4:25 p.m.

The afternoon Santa Ana winds have started moving in the clear sky brushing through the leaves of the maple and magnolia trees on the grassy spaces that line the side walk, creating a tranquilizing ambience, elicited by the sounds of small artificial waves crashing over head as the sound of a lawnmower running in the distance can be heard along with an occasional holler of, "Bang-bang, I got you!, You're dead!, You're dead!", of some of the kids in the neighborhood running around playing another game of "Search and Destroy." As violent as the name of the game suggests, they don't really destroy their enemy when they find them. But the "find and pretend to kill" name, didn't sound as cool as the one with destroy did. And calling it "army" lacked the pizzazz and influence the new name had to convince more kids to participate. This was a typical weekday afternoon on Carson street, Riverside, California, in this friendly small neighborhood of single family, track homes that had large grassy front yards separated only by low hedges, small picket fences or invisible property lines, and minimal car traffic making the playing field as spacious as the closest park which was about 4 miles from here. It is also where a young 21 year old homemaker, Amy Farrow lives with her 22 year old husband Luke and their only child, (9 month old baby, Steven).

With her shoulder length auburn hair tied back in a pony tail, dressed in an over sized blue sleeved baseball jersey undershirt, gray sweat pants and white tube socks, sporting her "Indoor Pony League Uniform" as she prefers to call the it, Amy, oblivious to the neighborhood kids running around outside, is in her house playing "coo-chi-coo" with her baby "Steven" who's laying on his back laughing, while she sits kneeling next to him and his stuffed brown teddy bear on the ruby red living room shag carpet. Baby Steven, dressed down, wearing only an undershirt and diaper; laughs then pauses with anticipation for his mommy to follow up with another face or claw attack on his little tummy, as she laughs back at him then stops like the game is over, then even though he's already expecting it he burst out with a scream of laughter as she gives him a tummy attack with her own face.

Though he still hasn't leaned how to walk or talk, Steven has a knack for crawling around quite fast and manages standing himself upright, balancing himself with one hand on the furniture or any other stable fixture he manages to crawl up next to. Often he lets go to tests his developing ability to stand unsupported, usually beating his previous time, by adding few more seconds to his record.

Recently, he learned that the kitchen trash container is occasionally loaded with what seems to be an unlimited resource of unpredictable goodies that are just there for the taking, and when mom isn't watching, he'll stand up next to it, pull the off the plastic lid, reach in, and take out whatever he gets his little hands on and tosses it all over the kitchen floor as fast as he can, making everything easier to sort through when he decides he's ready. It's terrific for passing the time until mom sees what he's up to and comes along and undoes all the progress he's made. Though he doesn't speak a common language he gets by, expressing himself his own way with his unknown language of baby gibberish that Amy seems to understand as most mothers would of their child. And sometimes when he's in a good mood, or casually preoccupied, he'll softly coo a made up tune or calmly speak the gibberish, as if he were reciting a poem.

As Amy continues playing with Steven, Fred Flintstone can be heard in the background talking with Barney Rubble, on the two dial, rabbit eared, RCA Color TV in the far corner of the room, playing to an audience of empty furniture. The familiar sounds of the cartoon serves as a time of day landmark and is a subtle reminder to Amy, that this is also her favorite time of day, being that all of her household chores are done, baby Steven has had his bath, and her husband Luke will be on his way home from work soon.

As the end credit music of the "The Flintstones" begins playing, Amy glances up at the clock on the wall and now she realizes that it's just a little later then she originally thought. The day was going so well and time just flew by, but now Luke could walk through the door any minute, and she realizes that she hasn't started preparing dinner, let alone consider what would be on the menu.

Picking Steven up, she switches off the TV, and carries him to the nursery, talking to him every step of the way. She once read in one of her baby rearing books that normal conversation stimulates learning and helps develop a stronger bond, so she makes it a point to try and eliminate dead air when she remembers, keeping a conversation going with Steven as much as possible by keeping him updated of what their next move is going to be. "OK, Sweetheart, it's time for your bottle... Do you want a bottle?... Sure you do..."

Modestly decorated in a Noah's Ark theme, the ark and animal figures that appear to be floating on the nursery sky blue walls have all been hand painted by Amy and Luke months before Steven was born. A yellow Tonka truck, red fire truck and a baseball mitt are on the floor with a couple of stuffed animals and an assortment of other baby toys near the back corner. As Amy walks in with Steven in her arms she purposely kicks a stray stuffed bunny that was in the middle of the room which rolls aside and stops perfectly among the group of other toys, .

Laying Steven in the crib, she hands him a baby teething toy that looks like a hoop of small bite size clear plastic cookies with even smaller colorful plastic figures in each cell floating in a clear fluid, melded together, which he gladly accepts, immediately puts to his mouth and begins chewing it. "There you go, baby," She cheerfully tells him, "Play with your ring, you're such a cutie, you are! Yes you are! Just look at you sweetheart! Now you wait right here, mommy's going to make your bottle... I'll be right back, OK."

As Amy leaves the room Steven tosses his
teething toy aside and he stands up using the crib
rail for support and almost starts to cry, but then he
suddenly stops when he notices a bag of balloons
that were left on top of the dresser next to his crib
and he takes a couple of steps towards the end of his
crib using the rails for support. He reaches for the
bag, grabs it, and plops back down on butt that's
reinforced by his cushy diaper.

Sitting in the middle of his crib, Steven examines
the bag. He recognizes little balloons but doesn't
really know how they work. He remembers seeing
mommy and daddy put them in their mouths and
they turn into big light weight balls. Steven searches
for an opening in the bag where he can pull out any
one of the small colorful treats he's determined to get
at.

From out of thin air, as silent as a flutter of a
butterflies wing, a beautiful ghostly woman with
blonde hair, wearing a flowing white dress, appears
before him. First looking around admiring the decor
of the room, then down at him, she smiles.

Preoccupied with the package of balloons in his
possession, Steven doesn't take any notice her, and
finally finding the opening in the bag, he pulls out a
single red balloon. Holding the deflated small red
rubbery morsel, it takes less than a second for him to
make the decision of what he should do next as he
moves his little hands towards his mouth. Then
suddenly before he can put the balloon in his mouth,
another hand larger and clearly too solid to belong to
the beautiful transparent ghost woman who's
standing directly before him, reaches in from behind
him and swaps it with the teething toy Steven had
tossed aside earlier. The exchange occurs so swift

and smooth, that Steven doesn't even realize what just happened, and he places the teething toy in his mouth. , Then realizing something isn't what it should be, he removes the teething toy and looks at it curiously, wondering for a moment what just happened? Although Steven still hasn't seen the man behind him, he hears his voice and that of the voice of the ghost woman standing before him. He doesn't understand what they're saying, so their conversation is of no significance to him. Uninterested in his teething toy Steven tosses it aside again and turns to his left and sees the beautiful ghost woman more clearly now and he smiles at her while she's talking. She stops talking and smiles back at him. His two front lower teeth have begun cutting through his gums over a month and a half ago and the uppers have just started, yet because they're still so small, they're barely visible as he flashes his big adorable smile.

The man he heard speaking moves around to the side of the crib where Steven can now see him. Wearing a light blue dress shirt and dark trousers, though he doesn't know who this man is he does looks somewhat familiar. The man moves around the crib to a standing position right next to the ghost woman and directs his attention to Steven and in the moment he and Steven make mutual eye contact, the two mysterious visitors vanish into thin air, just as silently as they appeared moments ago. The sudden disappearance of the two strangers right before his eyes, doesn't phase Steven in the least. As far as he was concerned, it really didn't matter much being that he didn't really know who they were anyway, and he turns his attention back to his crib and begins to play with a small toy stuffed animal.

A few second pass and Amy returns happily up
the hallway with the baby bottle in her hands. As she
approaches the room an inexplicable sensation
sweeps through her and grabs her attention
prompting her to stop in the doorway of the nursery.
As if she was suddenly paralyzed she quietly waits
still frozen like a statue in this position and listens
intently and with purpose looking in the room
focused on nothing but the invisible air just five feet
in front of her. A purpose unknown, for an event she
has never found herself confronted with ever before.
The strange feeling is miles beyond anything she has
ever felt before, tugging at her nerves and inner sense
of balance, triggering red flags and alarms that have
her petrified in fear and just a heartbeat away from
running in there, grabbing Steven and making a dash
out of the house as fast as she can. Nothing is visible
in the room or anywhere in the hall to indicate that
there should be any reason for this sudden fear or
suspicion, yet the angel and devil of consciousness
that rest on her shoulders are both convincing her
that something not of this world has just happened.
Something that somehow may have changed her
world forever. Like a Buckingham palace guard she
stands faithfully in her statue like posture holding
her breath, not moving a muscle, and listening to the
eerie silence that fills every corner, yet nothing visible
or audible presents itself. Then the silence is softly
broken by baby Steven cooing with his teething toy in
his mouth. Probably the only thing on earth that
could have done this, his cooing one of his made up
songs instantly eases her tension bringing her back
from out of the hypnotic trans that momentarily held
her captive. She turns her attention to Steven, who is
watching her through the wood bars of his crib. Now

relaxed with relief her demeanor transformed back to where it was just before she approached the doorway. The despair that stressed her magically and completely vanishes and she enters the room.

Looking baby Steven eye to eye and seeing his precious smile, makes her forget about the inexplicable intense anxiety that disheartened her just a moment ago and she feels her emotions rise up another three notches on the happy scale, as she walks to him with his bottle. "Oh boy! You're in such a good mood today. Just look at you sweetie!"

Steven tosses the teething toy aside takes hold of the bed rails and pulls himself up to a standing position and reaches out to Amy who hands him his bottle. He gladly take the bottle and Amy lays him down on his back as he begins drinking from his bottle looking contently into her eyes the entire time.

Resting her chin on her hands, on the bed rail, Amy looks down admirably at him, smiles and reaches through the wood bars and with her index finger she brushes his small knuckleless puffy baby soft hand holding his bottle. As if acknowledging her touch, Steven wiggles his little fingers softly without letting go of his bottle. Then she hears the front door open, close and Luke, calling from down the hall, in the living room, "Hello?... Amy?... Steven?...Where is everybody?"

Soon Luke appears at the open door of the nursery, smiling though his 5 o'clock shadow, and preceded by the feint odor of tire rubber from the shop where he works at. His dark brown hair is molded by the shape of the baseball cap he wears at work all day, and he's wearing work boots, jeans and a button up short sleeve shirt. "There you are," he says, as he walks in, kisses Amy on the cheek, then gives Steven a kiss and a big smile. "How's my little tank doing today?" he asks.

Still smiling and admirably looking down at Steven, she answers, "He's having such a good day. Right baby? He already had his bath... Oh!, and he's going to be walking all over the place, before you know it. He took four steps today!"

Steven sees his dad Luke, and pulls his bottle out of his mouth with a smack, then stands up to the bed rails beaming his big smile at him.

Being the proud father, Luke echoes Stevens latest accomplishment as he picks him up out of the crib. "Four steps, huh? That's my boy!"

"Aww, Luke, I just put him in there... If he gets fussy, you're dealing with it."

"That's OK, I can handle my little Steven. We're buddy's, right baby?" Holding baby Steven so that he's facing in Amy's direction, Luke says, "He says, he wants to pal with his daddy for a while."

"Luke, you smell like the shop you work in."

"Relax, babe. I'm gonna take a shower. I just want to have a little father and son time first."

Amy picks up Stevens' bottle from the crib and the three of them leave the nursery, Luke talking baby talk and playfully bumping heads with Steven as he carries him in his arms.

Chapter 2

April, 1984
Friday, 8:00 p.m.

8 years pass like the sands of time through an hourglass, each grain obeying the laws of nature and landing in their destined positions and buried by the flood of grains that follow. The night sky is calm, cool, and clear, and only the light of brightest stars and planets breaks through the fog of light pollution illuminating from the city below and the waning gibbous moon high above the horizon. Near the outskirts of town, Luke and Steven are at Scandia miniature golf park, which also features batting cages a go cart track, and a vast assortment of all the latest pinball machines, pool tables, air hockey and the newest video games. The amusement park is usually busy on Friday nights drawing large crowds, mostly teenagers and young adults. And with the miniature golf course and the indoor arcade drawing the bulk of customers, finding an available batting cage for a nice private practice session is no problem. That's where Luke and Steven are at the moment. It's where he knows he'll be able to coach Steven where he

won't be embarrassed if he messes up, and where he can encourage him with useful batting tips and prepare him for the upcoming little league baseball season.

Wearing his straight leg jeans a blue and white striped t-shirt, tennis shoes and the batting helmet supplied by the park, Steven stands poised with the aluminum bat Luke just bought for him earlier today. Waiting for the delivery of the pitching machine in the 40 MPH cage, Steven tries his best to connect with each pitch. He'll be turning 9 in a couple of months, and that'll make him just old enough to join the league this year, so this is the first time his parents let him sign up and he doesn't want to let them down. Right now he's feeling a little nervous from the burden of making this a successful outing. Regardless, he's determined to give it his best effort.

Steven's dad Luke anxiously watches from just outside the cage wearing his favorite baseball cap and coaching him between pitches. Luke, himself once wanted to be a professional baseball player. Back when he was Steven's age his parents signed him up to play in Little League and during his own free time he used to play ball with the other kids from the neighborhood and dreamed one day he would be a pro ball player, out on the perfectly manicured beautiful green field of grass, watched by a stadium full of admiring fans cheering him on. In high school he played for the school team and did well, but not good enough to secure a scholarship or draw interest from any scouts. After he finished high school he found work in a tire shop, saved up, married his high school sweetheart Amy, and not long after that, Steven was born. Since then, Luke's dreams of one day being a ballplayer faded as his priorities changed to providing a decent home and living conditions for his wife and child. Right now he's being cautious not to be overbearing on Steven. This is Steven's moment, he believes. And though success would be more than welcomed, it's not a do or die issue. Fun and learning love for the game is the most important thing he wants Steven to gain from all this. He knows Steven wants to play little league baseball because his friends at school are, and that's a big plus which he hopes will help Steven just relax and enjoy playing. Who knows? If he likes it enough, it might influence Steven to dream of being a professional ball player one day. "All right Steven, buddy, time the pitch! Time it! You can do it, babe!" Luke cheers him enthusiastically.

The green light flashes and the machine delivers the pitch. Steven swings and misses, as the ball slams into the padded fence behind him and bounces to the ground, rolling back, close to where he's standing. Although 40 miles per hour is the average pitching speed in the league he'll be playing in, batting against a machine is a whole new experience for him. This is his first time in the batting cage and it will take a little getting used to. "Wow, that was fast," Steven thinks to himself. But before he has time to concern himself about it, he hears his dad. And in spite the fact that he just completely missed the ball, Luke is cheering words of approval and encouragement.   Steven is embolden by his biggest fan and the best confidence builder a kid could hope for.

"That's OK, buddy! Hang in there! We'll get the next one! You can do it! You got the timing now! You can do it!"

The green light flashes, and the pitching

machine delivers another fast ball. It comes at him with the same smooth speed and the path it takes is right in the same strike zone as the previous pitch. Steven swings and connects right on the sweet spot, sending a slow line drive, just above the pitching machine.

The thrill of success and the rush of excitement hits Steven like a breath of fresh air causing him to almost lose his composure as goose bumps form on the back of his neck knowing he accomplished what he felt just a moment ago, a feat that seemed to be impossible. As excited as if it were a grand slam in the bottom of the ninth inning, of the seventh game of the World Series, Luke hollers, "Yes! That's it! Good hit! That's the way to go! Do it again Stevie!"

The adrenalin kicks in and Stevens heart races with excitement, but he maintains his self control as he stands poised and ready a stride of the home plate affixed to the concrete. As he waits in anticipation of the next pitch, the machine delivers once again and again Steven connects sending the ball flying up and over the machine. Luke cheers again. Unable to restrain himself further, Steven cracks a grin thinking to himself, this is the greatest day of my life!

*

The busy Friday night traffic of restless high school kids and young adults cruising has the street jammed with cars moving at 25 mph on the road leading from the amusement park to the freeway that Luke is trying to drive to. In the front passenger seat looking at a comic book is Steven, still floating on the thrill of the wave of happiness from his success in the recent battle of boy verses batting machine. If he had any doubts of his own abilities before, they're all gone now. I knew I could hit the ball, he thinks to himself. His past performances back at the school yard and playing with the kids in the neighborhood after school gave him the confidence that he could. But this was the first time Steven ever batted against a pitching machine and it provided a new boost of confidence that will help prepare him for playing in an organized League on a real team this year. I can't wait to tell mom, she'll be so excited when she hears how well I did, and though he's looking at a comic book his mind is clearly back at the batting cages and as he ponders he cracks a small grin. Then his train of thought is broken as the car picks up speed and his dad speaks, "Yes! Finally. We're moving now. I was beginning to think we would never get out of there. Feels good to be on the freeway and out of all that slow moving traffic.

Being on the freeway and away from the bumper to bumper traffic, Luke is able to let his guard down a little and relax as he drives. It also gives him room to talk freely with Steven. "You did real good out there, Son. I'm so proud of you."

Luke too, is riding on his own high of excitement, and cracks a smile every time he thinks of Steven hitting the ball. Then he thinks of the times when Steven missed a pitches and decides now is probably as good a time as any to provide advice that he hopes will help Steven out in the real game situation. "Don't worry about missing, son, just stay focused on how good it felt to hit that ball. And if it looks close to being a strike, go ahead and swing at it. You don't have to swing for the fence when it doesn't look like a perfect strike. Better to swing for a hit and protect the plate from something the umpire might call a strike. Better to strike out swinging then to have the umpire call you out looking," he says.

"Dad? What if the coach gives me a signal not to swing?," Steven asks.

"If you have two strikes and the coach signals you not to swing, call time out and check with him, you know..., to make sure you read his signal right. And if he still says not to swing then don't swing. He probably has a reason."

"I won't get in trouble for asking the coach in the middle of the game?"

"No, son. You shouldn't even worry about that. Don't be afraid to question something you don't understand. The questions you won't get answers to are the ones you never ask. And that's the difference between making a mistake and an error. An error is just a miscalculation or misjudgment of the direction or speed of the ball that permits the other teams runners to get on base, advance or even score points. A mistake is not knowing what to do to keep the other team in check, and possibly throwing the ball to a wrong teammate or something as simple as abandoning your post thinking there's three outs when in fact there was only two. It's something you can fix before it's made, just by staying alert and thinking before the play starts. So it's important to stay alert and focused. Like looking both ways before you walk across the street. Be smart, play smart. And if I know you Steven, you're a fart stinker." Luke shakes his head as if he just got slapped and corrects himself, "I mean smart thinker."

Steven let's out a small laugh at his dad's joke. His dad can be so funny at times. Usually when you least expect it. He could be talking about the most serious subject, then just when you think he's going to lose his temper or finalize what he's talking about with a serious point, he surprises you with an unexpected punch line.

"Dad, what if I make a lot of errors?," Steven asks.

"Maybe you will. You're still learning, son. Slip ups do happen. But don't let that bother you. Nobody's perfect. And remember, the errors you make won't always be your fault. Sometimes they're just unpreventable."

"So it's OK to make errors?," Steven asks.

"It's OK to make errors as long as you know you're playing the best you can son. The better you get at it, the less errors you'll make. That's why you practice. You'll get better with practice. And remember, even the greatest players in the world still make errors and strike out from time to time."

Steven thinks for a moment about his dad's advice. He never really thought much about the mental strategy in baseball before. He thought he knew the game as well as anyone needed to. At school, he could just go find his position and do his part as the game played out. Nobody ever really talked about mistakes being different from errors. In fact they didn't even call or count errors. The only thing that counted was how many runs were scored. And in the end the only thing that mattered was who scored more runs was the winner of the game. "Are you gonna come see all my games, Dad?" He asks,

"Well I don't know if I'll be able to make a promise that I'll be at all your games. But I can promise you that there's no place I'd rather be than right there watching you play. I'm gonna try, but I can't make any promises. Hey, you know what we should do if we get a chance? We should go see a real pro baseball game. Would you like that?"

"Yeah!"

"I'll talk to mom. I know she'll want to go. It'll be a lot of fun."

*

Luke pulls off the freeway and into a convenient store/gas station remotely located mostly for freeway travelers that might be passing through town. Pulling in under the gas station canopy, he parks the car with the rear passenger side next to the island of pumps closest to the store. With no other cars present, the station almost appears abandoned, which is not unusual for freeway gas stations at this time of night. A light mist of low hanging fog is visible out in an open field of undeveloped land located off in the distance behind the store which can be partially seen thanks to the bright lights emitted from the canopy. As he switches off the ignition key, Luke says, "I'll be right back, OK, Son. Stay in the car."

"OK dad." Steven answers, and returns to reading his comic book. Luke exits the car and goes into the store to pay for gas. As Luke enters the convenient store he casually greets the clerk making small talk just to be friendly, "Hi, how's it going." The clerk, (a young man in is twenty's, working alone, most likely moonlighting to make ends meet) appears to be either bored or tired. Either way courteous or friendly customer service isn't in his job description and the best he does is nod his head, and not to seem too rude he responds in a monotone voice, "It's quiet. Not too busy." Luke smiles still beaming with pride from how well the nights been going, "Ah, $20 on number 3, please." The clerk takes the $20 and the smile he notices on Luke's face infects him like a virus and he cheers up a little. He presses the buttons that activates pump 3, and tells Luke, "Your all set. Have a good night." Still smiling, Luke says, "Thank you" and heads for the exit. As he exits through the front door, he passes by another man, who's on his way in. He doesn't take any notice of the man who eyes Luke up and down rather intently as if he were about to ask him something important but doesn't bother and just continues his own way into the store.

As Luke Walks toward his car, he see's Steven sitting in the front seat reading his comic book, and notices a smile, an expression of happiness and solemn content on Stevens' face that makes himself feel even better about today. It makes the smile he's been wearing since he left the amusement park grow a little bit more. He still finds it amazing how one little person can bring in so much happiness into his life. When he married Amy he felt she completed his life. Who knew there was so much more room for happiness in his heart to be released through sharing love for a child. I have the perfect family, he thinks to himself, when I get home I'm going to give Amy a big kiss just to thank her for making my life what it is today. He removes the gas cap and slides the pump nozzle into the tank opening above the passenger side rear tire and squeezes the handle and sets the trigger lock to automatically pump the gas. Just then he notices the clerk in the store with his hands up and he moves a little towards the back of his car where he can get a better view of what's happening. As he watches the robbery taking place he focuses on details of what the thief looks like and the clothes he's wearing so he'll be able to provide an accurate

description to the police. As he watches from the
back of his car another car pulls into the station just
behind him.

Sitting in the front seat of the car, Steven is
looking at his comic book when he notices the other
car pulling in out on the driver side, driven by a
woman. The car she's driving is a four door sedan
which she pulls up to the gas pumps to his left facing
the opposite direction. Then he looks to his right, out
his window towards the convenient store just in time
to see a man violently pushing open the front door
and rush out through it with a gun in one hand and
a bag in the other. It's obvious the man just robbed
the store and is hurrying to get away. At first Steven
is a little thrilled by the action and the idea that it's
all happening right here and he's got a front row seat.
The man clumsily stumbles as he bumps a trash can
anchored right by the front door, and a stray cat
darts out from behind it. Then he trips over the cat
and falls to the ground. At first all the stumbling and
falling to the ground makes Steven start to laugh but
then as suddenly as it seemed funny, the situation
became serious as the clumsy bad guy squeezes the
trigger and gun in his hand fires. Steven sees the
flash of fire from the muzzle of the gun and hears the
blast of the gunshot a micro second after, intensified
as it echoes down from the metal soffit of the canopy
and back up from the smooth concrete driveway. The
loud blast from the gunfire causes Steven to wince.
Steven can't believe this is all happening right before
his eyes. He never saw a gun fire with a flash
shooting out from the muzzle like that, outside from
the movies or on television. My friends won't believe
me when I tell them all this, he thinks. With a
frightened look on his face the man nervously and

quickly picks himself up and runs toward the back of the store, jumps in a parked car, starts it and drives away. Steven doesn't know what kind of car it is, only that it's a plain white car that looks like a hundred others that he's seen on the road.

Steven looks back at the front door of the store and sees the store clerk holding one hand on his nose that looks a little bloody, and in the other he's holding a phone to his ear, probably calling the police. The store front is all glass so most of what's happening throughout the inside of the store can be seen from the street. Still looking in the store, Steven notices two figures inside, near the spot where the robber fell to the ground out front. One of them is a man wearing a light blue, long sleeve dress shirt who appears to be weeping with his hands covering his face, and the other a ghostly transparent looking woman with long flowing blonde hair, wearing a white dress standing next to him. The fact that she appears to be a ghost causes Steven to wonder if any of what just happened is real. Tough she is transparent he is able to make out the fact that she is beautiful, and though at this young age in his life Steven isn't into girls yet, her beauty draws his interest like no girl has ever before. She appears to be whispering to the man who appears to be crying. Steven doesn't know why, but the beautiful ghost woman looks familiar to him. She looks like someone he's seen before, but he doesn't know from where. He looks back at the clerk who is still on the phone then back to where the man and the ghost lady were standing, but now they're gone. A quick scan of the store shows no evidence of them anywhere in the store. Then he quickly turns around and looks to the back of the car to see if his father is witnessing the same thing he did. His dad is not visible anywhere at the back of the car.

Steven nervously looks left and right searching for his dad, but doesn't see him anywhere. His dad told him to stay in the car but this is different. This is like an emergency. Cautiously, he opens the car door and slowly steps out walking to the rear of the car where at first he sees the gas pump hose leading to the nozzle in the car, no longer pumping gas. Then he sees the car gas cap on the ground and tears start welling in his eyes as he fears the worst. When he reaches the gas pump hose he sees his dad face down on the ground behind the car, and he takes a deep breath releasing a quiet gasp. Voice cracking, he's barely able to get the word out of his mouth without breaking down and crying.

"...Dad?"

*

No siren but with red and blue lights flashing, a police car pulls into the gas station and parks near the front door of the store. Two uniformed policemen hurriedly get out of the car and both of them start for the front door. The officer who was riding shotgun makes his way into the store but the driver stops frozen in his tracks at the front of the patrol car as he happened to glance to his left, out at the gas pumps and is saddened by what he sees. Luke's lifeless body is lying on the ground face down at the back of his car, blood pooling at his right side, and to the left of him is a woman in tears, standing with her baby in one arm and her other hand resting on Steven's shoulder as he kneels by his fathers side weeping with his hands over his face.

Chapter 3

It was almost a week before the medical examiner released Luke's body. Then the mortuary needed a couple more days to be ready for the funeral service and burial. Steven is exhausted from going to bed crying every night and waking up in the middle of the night from dreams of being out with his dad that turn into nightmares of his dad either getting killed or just disappearing and leaving him alone out in the middle of town all alone to fend for himself.

At the funeral his mom, grandparents and relatives as well as some of his fathers closest friends were in tears, sobbing as a few speakers stood up and testified how a good brother and friend Luke was, and spoke of good times or shared funny stories of things that happened in the past. All Luke wanted, was for the political sideshow to end, hoping and praying that the whole funeral service wasn't real and maybe he would just wake up from what he wanted to believe was just the worst nightmare of his life. The thought of bragging to his friends about being at the gas station and witnessing the store robbery and seeing the gun fire, lost it's thrill to the fact that it all led to his dad being killed. He didn't want to talk about it. The thought that he found it exciting at first loaded him with guilt and regret. He often tried to play out the events as they happened trying to make something different happen, that would end with his dad not being dead in the end.

After the funeral friends and family gathered at Luke's grandmothers home for a lunch buffet that was prepared and donated by the women's auxiliary group from her church. Steven is still grieving and has been moping around sadly since he arrived, excusing himself to the bathroom so he could let out a quiet sob occasionally. The past seven days have been so very difficult for him. His internal clock has been thrown completely off kilter, from the broken sleep and silent depression. His mother, Amy has been crying with him on and off, everyday since Luke died. At times she seemed so much stronger than Steven and reassured him that everything was going to be OK and that his father was in heaven and one day they would all be reunited. But even with the promise of seeing him again one day, all Steven can think of was how much he misses his dad. And how his dad will never be around anymore to share in the good times from here on out. Nothing will ever be as fun as it would've been if his dad was here.

Steven goes into the den and sits at the end of the couch with his Uncle Mark and uses one of the small pillows to rest his head. Uncle Mark, Luke's brother, is watching The Price Is Right on TV, and trying to guess the prices of common household products and criticizing the contestants when he's in disagreement with them. He never noticed it before, but Uncle Mark looks a little like Luke, and Steven admires the resemblance and for a moment he sees his dad, then he sees Mark again. Steven watches the show on the TV in a daze staring right through the screen to the point where it starts to appear blurry, 3D, blurry, 3D, blurry then he tiredly falls asleep.

The sound "ding, ding, ding, ding..." from the TV show, rings repeatedly waking him up as he sees on the TV that a contestant just won a lot of money. He notices that Uncle Mark is gone and nobody else is in the room with him and he gets up and goes out to the dining room where he hears everybody talking but he doesn't see anyone. "Hello?" Steven calls out, "Where is everybody?"

Nobody answers.

"Hey!... Where did everyone go?!!"

Steven looks around as he hears the voices surrounding him in the room, but he still doesn't see anyone, and an uncomfortable fear is beginning to bother him. What's going on here? If this is a joke, it isn't funny. Not even remotely funny. He goes into the living room and sees a beautiful woman dressed in a white gown standing by the couch. He doesn't know her, but she does look familiar.

"Who are you?" he asks.

"Hi Steven. I am Raziel."

"Where did everybody go?"

"There at your grandmas house."

"This is my grandmas house."

"This is your dream."

"My dream?" Steven asks while looking around. Though he's unable to make out what it is their saying or talking about, the voices of everyone talking is still audible.

"I'm dreaming this?"

"Yes. Close your eyes and think of someplace else."

Steven closes his eyes and the voices go silent. Opening his eyes he finds himself standing atop a mountain, looking down at the town he lives in. The sun has just set on the distant mountain horizon and the clouds and the sky to the west are glowing red creating a beautiful backdrop to the local mall and all the houses within view. As Steven sits and admires the natural beauty created by the blending of night and day, half the sky quickly darkens even more and though he's still depressed about his fathers death, and he's momentarily distracted from his grief and thinks to himself how cool it would be if he were to see a falling star right now.

Then it happens. A shooting star zips silently across the darker part of the sky and vanishes into the amber glow in the west. Then another following along the same path. He closes his eyes tightly as if to make a wish and when he opens them he sees Raziel standing next to him and now he takes more notice of what she looks like. She doesn't have a single blemish, mole, or freckle on her perfect complexion, nor does she have a hair out of place in her silky smooth blonde hair. Her eyes appear hazel in color but change to blue when she's looking directly at you. She looks familiar to Steven, who gets the feeling he's seen her before but for the life of him, he doesn't remember from where. She looks nothing like any of his relatives or any of his teachers from school or ladies from the church he attends. Yet he feels like she's not someone he just met, but instead someone he's known for a while. As beautiful as she is he doesn't find himself attracted to her like a girlfriend but instead he feels a family closeness to her as if she were a his grandmother, or an aunt.

"How do you know me?" he asks.

"I'm an angel. I hope we can be friends."

Upon hearing that she's an angel, Steven tries to lean in for a closer look at her back, searching for wings, but he doesn't see any. Nor does he see a halo hovering above her head.

"Looking for something?" she says, and as if she were reading his mind, large white dove-like feathered wings fan out behind her with the sound like that of a parachute opening up and catching the wind, causing Steven to flinch back nervously.

"You don't need to be frightened," she says, as the wings quietly retract behind her back and disappear entirely.

Remembering the shooting stars he saw, Steven asks, "Are you going to make my wishes come true?"

Raziel smiles at the thought of how people make wishes on falling stars, blowing on dandelions, or whatever they may have been taught. "No Steven. It doesn't work that way. I'm here in your dreams to help you understand a few things."

With an angel standing before he remembers about his father. Maybe this is his chance to get some answers to a question he's been praying about. "Can you tell me why my dad had to die?" he asks.

Raziel knows there's more to Gods plan than what's been revealed to her. She's here armed only with knowledge to help Steven understand what is happening in his dreams. Any explanation of "why things happen" is beyond what she was sent to do. Steven must learn those things on his own, and only when he chooses to do so.

"One day you may understand why, Steven. Trust me. Right now there's nothing more I can tell you about that."

Getting upset Steven lashes back with tears welling in his eyes, "It's not fair! He was the best dad in the world!"

Raziel knows his loss is devastating to him, and right now the pain he's going through is one that only he could know. Eventually his grief will fade as he learns to live with his loss. She also knows that Luke is in a better place, and that is something that Steven can only understand if he believes.

"I'm sure he was," she says, "But you need to be strong Steven... Live... Enjoy your life. Your father would have wanted that. You have friends and family that are waiting for you to come back and be a part of their life."

Still angry, Steven says, "I'm not going to play little league baseball."

"Don't stop doing the things you enjoy, Steven. But it doesn't matter whether you choose to play in sports or not. What's more important is that you don't forget what you father taught you. Remember to keep God's love in your heart. As long as you have that, you will have the strength to make it through these days and the hard times that may lie ahead."

Raziel rests her right hand on Steven's shoulder and closes her eyes as a glow emits from her body. Steven looks up at the sky and thinks to himself that if there's an angel here talking to him, his dad must be in heaven. "Raziel, I don't know why but I feel better. Am I gonna see you again?" he asks.

There are conditions set that won't allow her to reveal her identity beyond the world of dreams. Not to

Steven or any other human.

"I'm sure we'll meet again. You will always recognize me in your dreams, but when you are awake you will have no memory of me. When you wake up, the talks we have, you will remember as if they were your own thoughts, in your own mind. Kind of like if I were your subconscious."

Kind of confused, Steven asks, "So I'm gonna forget all this?"

"You won't forget any of this. But like I said, you will remember our talks, as if they were your own thoughts. And my existence, you will never know outside of your dreams."

"Why won't I remember you when I'm awake?"

"Trust me , my identity wouldn't serve you any purpose in your world, Steven."

Steven wakes up from his dream, and he's back in the den on his grandmas couch, sitting next to his Uncle Mark, who's still watching The Price Is Right on the TV. He doesn't remember anything except being at the top of a mountain, seeing the beautiful sky, and thinking to himself that his dad is in heaven, and that he, "himself" needs to be strong and keep doing the things he enjoys in life. He remembers everything from his dream but not the angel Raziel.

There are still relatives visiting. Some will probably spend the night and make their long drive home tomorrow. Although it's still early in the day, he's tired and hungry from what seems like the longest day ever to him, so he gets up and goes for something to eat from the buffet set up in the kitchen.

Chapter 4

September, 1984
3:00 p.m.

Five months have past since the funeral and
Steven is now 9 years old. Following what seemed like
a hot day, the afternoon breeze feels good on the back
of Stevens neck as he walks Skipper, his grandmas
pet dog, up the sidewalk. Skipper is poodle terrier
mix mutt who kind of looks like Benji the famous TV
dog star from Petticoat Junction. He was given to
Grandma Lee by a friend from church about a year
ago when he was just a puppy, who began his stay
here as an indoor dog, and gradually wound up
spending more time as a back yard dog with his own
little dog house during good weather. And during bad
weather such as thunder storms or in the winter
when it got real cold, Grandma Lee would bring
Skipper into the house and bathe him washing away
all the outdoor dirty dog smell and converting him

into an indoor dog.

Steven casually strolls up the sidewalk towards Grandma Lees house with Skipper leading the way tugging on his leash. As they both arrive to the front yard, instead of making their way up the steps of the front porch, they both veer off to the left side of the house and through the gate and along the walkway at the side of the house and to the back yard.

Stopping at the back door, Steven kneels down and tries to remove Skippers leash from his collar but he's having a very difficult time trying to undo the rusted hook release. Skipper doesn't make matters any easier as he keeps tugging on his leash and nipping at Steven as he struggles with it. He tries for a good ten minutes before he finally gives up and releases Skipper who has also had enough of the senseless tugging on his collar, and scampers away. Steven watches Skipper run about the backyard with the leash dragging behind him for a moment then he goes into the house to tell Grandma Lee about Skippers stuck leash.

When Steven walks in the house, he's misdirected by the urge to relieve himself, and instead of telling Grandma Lee about the jammed hook release on Skippers leash he heads straight for the bathroom. After relieving himself, Steven comes out of the bathroom and he hears a familiar cartoon playing on the TV in the living room. The cartoon playing on the TV is a rerun that he remembers watching before and it draws his interest to the point where he completely forgets about Skippers leash stuck to his collar, and he sits down in front of the TV immersed in the program.

Out in the back yard, Skipper's leash dragging from his collar doesn't phase him, as he explores along the perimeter fence line. Searching and sniffing the ground as if he were impersonating bloodhound tracking an escaped convict on the run, he pauses and lifts a hind leg to relieve himself then he spots a gopher along the side of the house away from its hole. Skipper lets out a gruff and makes a dash for the gopher who's suddenly startled and caught off guard instead of running towards his hole which would bring him closer to Skipper he away in the opposite direction along the side of the house, which happens to be a late model Victorian built in the early 1900's, and sits elevated on a foundation about 18 inches above ground level. The fleeing gopher finds a small opening by way of a tear in a vent screen panel and goes through it, under the house. Determined not to lose him that easy, Skipper easily pushes his head through the opening and eventually works his front paws through, then the rest of his body which is a struggles at first but he makes it through with his leash still dragging behind him. His leash gets caught on the wire mesh screen for a moment and stops Skipper with a sudden yank, but he tugs on it a couple of times until it breaks loose.

Under the house Skipper has lost sight of the gopher and tries to sniff the powdery dirt under the house like a blood hound and instead of finding a scent to follow he gets just enough dust in his nostrils to make him sneeze. Now having lost interest in looking for the untraceable rodent Skipper finds himself intrigued with the shaded world he's in. He explores further inward, till he comes around a foundation pylon near the center of the house and his leash gets caught on a nail in a foundation form post that was left anchored deep into the ground long ago during original construction. Skipper pulls and tugs on the leash attached to his collar which only gets tighter and more tangled as he circles around the anchored post to a point where he can move no more. He sits and pants nervously keeping a tight tension on his leash as if in doing so maybe the post that holds him captive would get tired and surrender and release him. Poor Skipper begins to whimper as he now knows he's trapped under the house by his own leash, and nobody knows he's here.

*

4:00 p.m.

Inside the house, Amy sits down with the afternoon newspaper at the dining room table next to "Grandma Lee" who's crocheting, while Steven sits mesmerized on the front living room floor by the antics of Bugs Bunny being chased around a large ship by the pirate Yosemite Sam, when there's a knock at the front door. Without taking his eyes off the TV, Steven gets up to answer the door. It's Eddie, one of Steven's friends who lives a couple of houses down the street .

Eddie is 9 years old. And though he and Steven don't attend the same school, they've been close friends of this neighborhood for over three years, and since Luke died Amy has been spending a lot more time visiting her mother then she used to when Luke was alive.

"Hey, Steven. Can you come out and play?" Eddie asks.

Steven looks back to where his mom and grandma are and asks, "Mom, can I go out and play?"

"Sure sweetie, don't go anywhere too far, were having dinner in about an hour. OK?"

"Ok."

Steven turns the TV off and hurries out the door.

"And don't slam the door!" She says, just as the door slams behind Steven as he scurries out through the front porch. Muffled through the closed door Steven can be heard calling back, "Sorry!"

Amy shakes her head and looks back down at the newspaper spread on the dining room table as Grandma Lee continues crocheting what appears to be a small tea cozy. Then Amy breaks the silence commenting on the article she's reading about, with a hint frustration in the tone of her voice, "Guilty of involuntary manslaughter."

The thief who accidentally shot Luke, turned himself in the very next morning when he heard that Luke died. He had no intention of killing anyone when he robbed the store. Had the clerk was slow to open the cash register and he punched him in the nose to put the scare in him not to try and do anything to stop him. Killing anybody was never an option. Not even as a backup plan. He knew the gun was loaded. When he bought it a few years ago, loading it was the first thing he did. And the practice at the firing range gave him the confidence that he would be able to pull the job off without a hitch. If he had to shoot anyone, it would be a shot in the thigh, a wound that would heal in time. But only as a last resort. He was so nervous about committing the crime when the ball started rolling, he didn't even consider checking the gun to make sure the safety was engaged after he grabbed the cash. When he heard from a friend that Luke died from the stray bullet, he was so overwhelmed with guilt and fear that he felt his best and only defense would be to turn himself confess that the shooting was accidental and throw himself on the mercy of the court, hoping they would give him a lesser sentence and take into consideration the fact that he's never committed any serious crimes prior to this.

At first the DA wanted to take him down with murder in the first degree. He saved himself from that by turning himself in the way he did. And it didn't take long to come to the conclusion that the chances of getting a conviction of murder was very slim. His attorney didn't even need to convince him to plea guilty to involuntary manslaughter. No jury trial was required. The investigation convinced the DA that the situation couldn't even be considered as an aggravated robbery escape. All the evidence showed the killing to be accidental. Knowing what the charges were, Amy saw no reason for attending any of the hearings, but the DA's office kept her informed and she read the local paper just to keep informed of what was happening.

"Does it say how long he's gonna be in jail?" Grandma Lee responds, without missing a stitch.

"It says manslaughter crimes get 4 to 15 years max, but this is a first time offense for him, so the judge will probably give him between 4 and 8."

Grandma Lee stops crocheting and looks to Amy with concern. Luke's dying so tragically was heartbreaking for her, and all she wanted was to do was forget about what happened and remember Luke for the son he was to her and the happiness he brought. Like Amy, at first she had intended to be in court everyday of the trial till she learned that he had confessed to the shooting and cut a deal. "It isn't fair. First he ends Luke's life, changes our world forever, gets 4 to 8 years in prison then he's back out on the streets, like nothing ever happened," she says.

Amy closes the newspaper and stares blankly. "I don't know why I bother reading this crap," she says.

"Amy!, Language."

"Sorry mom. It just makes me so angry. Why do I even read this stuff?"

"You're reading it, because like the rest of us, you want to know that this man gets punished for what he did. This awful person hurt all of us. He took away the man we all loved. Your husband, my son. And even poor little Steven has to grow up without his father. You're right dear. The punishment their giving him isn't enough."

Grandma Lee goes back to crocheting the tea cozy and Amy just stares down at the newspaper on the table, then folds it shut and looks out the window from where she sits. They both sit quiet for a moment, till Grandma Lee says, "How is my little Steven doing at home?"

"He's been taking this just as hard as me. Poor little thing, didn't want to play little league baseball anymore. I wonder sometimes if he's just doing it for me. But he says he really doesn't want to play, and I can't force him to play. Then he says it's his job to take care of me, helps out around the house with things."

"What do you mean? What kind of things?"

"You know, the usual stuff, he keeps his room clean and helps out with all the chores. Even the dishes and the laundry. I appreciate all the help, but sometimes it seems a little excessive. I hope it's just a phase. I'm telling you it's kind of nice to see him go outside and play with the neighborhood kids."

Grandma Lee echoes' her sentiments, "Poor thing. He's such a sweet little boy. I couldn't imagine what it must be like to be so young and go through what he's gone through."

*

    Most of the front yards in the neighborhood where Grandma Lee lives have sidewalks leading up to the front porches through nice size lawns with fully grown trees and shrubs or flower beds on the property lines that divide neighboring yards. Scattered clouds overhead have been blocking the sun on and off and an afternoon breeze has made the day cooler and pleasant for the game of hide and seek the kids are about to play. Steven, Lisa, Eddy, Cindy and Robin have all agreed to use the tree in Grandma Lee's front yard as home base. Cindy loses the (one potato, two potato, three potato, four) draw which makes her the first one it. As the other three kids run about looking for their hiding places, she counts, eyes closed, forearms crossed over her face and leaning towards the tree, "5, 10, 15, 20, 25, 30...100. Apples, peaches, pumpkin pie, who's not ready holler aye!" No one responds and Cindy sets out in search of the hiding playmates.

    Steven has found himself a cool hiding spot not far from the home base tree on the opposite side of the yard. From where he is, he could easily outrun Cindy to the tree, if only her quest takes her far enough away from it. In an case he finds the game just as fun to wait in his hiding place to be discovered, and take on the challenge of the race back to the tree designated as home base. And if he doesn't get found, that would be even more rewarding, and achieving victory through not being discovered. He crouches low behind a hedge that divides his grandmas and Lisa's house, right at the point where it meets the chain link fence that divides his grandmas front and backyard. As he waits in his hiding place enjoying the fact that Cindy hasn't shown any hint that she has any idea where he is, he happens to glance through the fence into the back yard and notices a strange man wearing a long sleeve light blue shirt and black pants with his back turned, standing about 60 feet away. The stranger looks like he could be a relative of his late father Luke. In fact he even looks a little like his dad from behind, as if his dad had another brother that he never new about. The idea of his dad having a brother he never knew about seems impossible. Even Grandma Lee would have mentioned a him at one time or another. Steven doesn't no of any reason why this man or any other should be in his grandmas back yard, and he's planning on telling his grandma about him just as soon as gets out from this hiding spot. But in the meantime he decides to keep watching to see what he's up to. Still unable to see the mans face, he does notice that it appears as if the man is speaking to himself. Then he sees Skipper come around the corner from behind the house, and he remembers that Skipper had his leash stuck to his collar the last time he saw him. But now the leash is not attached to his collar. Skipper trots towards the man like nothings wrong, as if he knows the man, and when he reaches him, he stops, sits and just looks up at a position next to the stranger. The man takes a knee and pets Skipper, who is casually receptive to the gesture. Skipper has taken to this stranger the way he would a close member of the family.

Steven focuses concentrating on the position where skipper's looking at next to the man and a transparent image of a beautiful ghost woman with

long blonde hair, wearing a flowing white gown begins
to appear. She looks just like the woman he thought
he saw at the gas station the night his father was
killed, but he's not sure. Then he starts to wonder if
these two people maybe had something to do with the
robbery that took place. Or maybe they had
something to do with his fathers death and now
they're here for the rest of his family. He sees her face
clearly now, and something about it doesn't seem
real. She looks too perfect. As if she were a movie star
but not wearing a ton of makeup. She sees him, and
she's saying something that Steven can't hear. Then
the man turns around to look at Steven, and just as
Steven makes eye contact with the stranger, the man
and the ghost woman vanish in thin air.

Skipper gets up as if nothing unusual has just
happened, and trots off to the back yard. Steven
stands up in a temporary state of shock. They were
both ghost, he thinks to himself. Or were they spirits
from another dimension. The man seemed to
disqualify himself as the grim reaper when he pet
Skipper and he didn't die. Standing and staring into
the back yard, Steven gives away his position and
Cindy immediately spots him, runs up and tags him.
"I got you Steven!... Steven's it!, Steven's it!"

Chapter 5

At bedtime Steven lays in bed and reflects on what happened out in his grandmas backyard earlier that afternoon. The thought of having seen a ghost was scary enough, but when he saw the man disappear and realized that he saw two ghosts, that made it even more unsettling. Just thinking about how he didn't even know that the man was a ghost from the start and all of it happening in broad daylight seemed so incredible. How many times has he seen a ghost and not known it?

Steven thinks back to the ghost woman. Why did she look so familiar? He wonders to himself. Reaching deep into his memory and narrowing his search to all the women he remembers ever meeting or crossing paths with, seen in movies, on TV or in magazines, he doesn't draw a single match. Nor can he recall anyone who even resembles her. Yet the thought that he knows her from somewhere, lingers as if he were not being completely true to himself. And the more women he tries match her with, the more his memory of what she looks like fades away.

Of course none of the other kids really believed him when he tried to tell them what he had seen. Why should they? By the time he told them what he saw, all proof was gone and nobody else could back up his story. Had Skipper stayed put, it might of provided some credibility. But before he could even recover from the shock of it all and bring himself around to explain, Skipper had already left the scene. The closest it seemed that any of them were starting to believe what he was saying, was when Cindy and Lisa were beginning to appear frightened and concerned. Then Robin remembered some urban myth ghost stories he felt like sharing which made the encounter seem even more made up, as the conversation moved in the ghost story trading time.

Steven keeps wondering to himself what he should've done that would've made the rest of the gang believe him. Without anyone to back up what he saw, he decided not to tell his mom or Grandma Lee. Thinking about how he knows what he saw, but doesn't have any way to prove it, he tiredly falls asleep and begins to dream.

*

His dream takes him back in the same batting cage he and his father visited the last night they were together. Steven stands ready for the machine to deliver, as he glances at the speed control and sees that it's set for 80 miles per hour. Realizing that he's never batted against the machine with the speed set so high his eyes widen with fear, but it's too late to back out as the green light flashes and the ball is sent speeding towards him. Steven swings and to his own surprise, he makes perfect contact sending the ball he hit flying up and away at the perfect angle, as he thinks to himself, that would've been a home run. Then hears his dad cheer from behind just outside the cage.

"Yes! That's it! Good hit! That's the way to go! Do it again Stevie!"

Dad's here!, he thinks to himself. But he is unable to turnaround and look back because the machine sets up to deliver another pitch. The green light flashes again as like an instant replay, Steven swats the ball perfectly sending it flying along the same path as the one before it. This time instead of hearing his dad cheer he hears Raziels' soft voice right next to him, "Nice hit, Steven."

Steven turns to look. And standing at the spot where a catcher would be if this were a real game is Raziel. Right behind home plate, where a pitching machine is firing 80 mph fast balls to a hitter with as little experience as himself, Steven knows standing there isn't the best idea. Sooner or later he's bound to swing and miss, allowing the speeding ball to hit her.

"Raziel...You can't stand there! You'll get hit by the ball!" he yells. Just then the green flashes again and another pitch is sent speeding towards them. Steven swings and hits the ball perfectly, returning the speeding ball in a straight line drive directly over the pitching machine.

"Raziel! You have to move! You're gonna get hit!" Steven yells.

Raziel knows she has nothing to worry about in Stevens dream. Even if Steven were to miss the ball it would just pass right through her as if she were just an illusion within his dream. She told Steven when they first met, she's here to help him understand some things, but she isn't prepared for is the fact that some things have already happened that she doesn't readily understand herself.

"Steven, you're dreaming," she tells him.

Not having given much thought about where he is, how he got here, why he would have clearly heard his dads' voice, or the fact that he's talking to an angel, Steven thinks for a second and realizes what she's telling him must be true. But he remains poised and ready to hit the next pitch.

"What?" he asks.

She tells him again, "You're dreaming."

Steven, looks carefully at the pitching machine and it becomes more clear to him that it's not turned on. Nothing is. All the lights are off, and the facility is closed. If not for the moonlight shining down from above it would be totally dark here. And he realizes now that he's not even holding a bat.

Remembering that he heard his dads cheer from just outside the batting cage, he looks back behind Raziel, but there's no sign of him. Everything shutting down and becoming quiet so suddenly reminds him of how quickly his father was taken from him. Luke was always there for him and mom. There was still so much to look forward to. So much fun left to be had. Then in the blink of an eye. Just as fast as the lights going out just now, it all shut down. Nothing left but a closed arcade. Fading images of how nice things were. It wasn't due to negligence on his or his dads part. His dad was doing all the right things. He was taken too soon. We didn't do anything wrong. Why did he die? Steven thinks to himself.

"Raziel. I miss him so much."

"I know Steven. Sometimes your dreams bring you here just because you're thinking of him. It's good you have this place to remember him."

Looking at Raziel Steven suddenly remembers what he saw earlier that day in his grandmas back yard. The man and the ghost woman... yes the ghost woman!

"Raziel, I saw you today at my grandmas house!"

Raziel has no recollection of ever being at Stevens grandmas house. And wonders for a moment, how that could possibly be true.

"I don't remember being at your grandma's house today," She says.

"It was you. You're the ghost woman! I know it was you! And you were talking to a man."

"A man?"

Forgetting what Raziel told him about not knowing her in his world Steven is a little confused. "I didn't I remember you when I saw you though? I know now it was you. But when I saw you today, I didn't recognize you," he tells her.

"You will only recognize me in your dreams, Steven."

Still confused, Steven asks, "What were you doing at my grandma's house today?"

"I don't know. I don't remember being there."

"How could you not remember? It just happened earlier today."

"I don't know, Steven. I don't know of any man you speak of. You're the only human I can speak with. I'm not sure what's going on? Or what I was doing at your grandmas house today."

"But you're an angel, aren't you supposed to know everything?"

"Steven... just because I'm an angel, that doesn't mean I know everything. I'm only here to help you understand your dreams, remember. You weren't dreaming when you were at your grandma's house today, so I don't know how or why you saw me."

"So who was that man with you?... Was he a relative of my dad?" Steven asks.

"I don't know who he was. Like I said I don't remember ever being there."

"He kind of looked like my dad. Is it possible that was him?"

"He wasn't your father, Steven."

"Is it possible that it wasn't you I saw today?" he asks.

"No. That's impossible," she tells him, "If it were someone else you saw, you would know now it wasn't me. It's possible for you to mistake people for other people. But you could never mistake a person or another angel for being me. If you say it was me that you saw, then it must've been me."

"Then why don't you remember it?"

"I don't know, Steven. Right now it doesn't even make any sense to me."

"I thought it was your job to help me understand my dreams."

"Steven, you weren't dreaming when you saw me today. And I can't explain what's happening to you in your world."

Steven remembers how frightened he was when he saw the man and Raziel in his grandmas back yard and asks, "Raziel... why's this happening? Should I be scared? I know I was earlier today."

Still not sure herself, about what's happening Raziel tells Steven, "Don't worry, Steven. You won't forget what you saw today. But I'm sure, one day, we'll both understand what happened, and who that man was."

Raziel and the batting cage fade away as Steven's

dream takes him to a different time and place. He's now in an imaginary classroom, sitting at a desk taking a test he isn't prepared for. Looking at the clock on the wall he sees that time is almost up and he hasn't even started. Then he notices that he's dressed in nothing but underwear. None of the other students are even phased by the fact that he isn't wearing clothes, but he's still dying of embarrassment wondering how he's going to get out of this strange predicament. Then the school bell rings, and Steven wakes up to the ringing bell his own alarm clock back home safe in bed.

Chapter 6

November.
9:45 a.m.

Wearing her robe over a sleep gown, Grandma Lee is in the kitchen finishing up with the morning post breakfast cleaning routine. Having finished washing the dishes, she wipes her hands dry with a dish towel when she notices Steven in the front living room, sitting on the floor, watching Saturday morning cartoons. At first it strikes her as a bit odd because she was pretty sure that the TV was off just a moment ago and that nobody else was here in the house with her. She thought Steven had left with his mom to pick up her prescription and a few things at the local drug store, but evidently she must have been mistaken.

"Steven... Stevie, honey."

Steven stands up and looks at Grandma Lee. He appears slightly confused and disoriented but doesn't say anything. He just curiously looks at her in a daze as if she'd suddenly caught him off guard.

"I thought you went with your mom to the store?" She asks.

"No... I'm here," Steven says, but still looking somewhat confused.

"Do you want something to snack on, maybe a peanut butter and jelly sandwich or something?"

"Sure Grandma."

"OK," she says, as she goes to the cupboard and retrieves the peanut butter.

Something seems odd to Steven. He's not quite sure what it is. But something is definitely out of whack here. Looking nervous, he walks over to his grandmother, who is now fixing his sandwich.

When he reaches the kitchen and is standing right next to her, he nervously extends his hand and touches her forearm, as if he were testing for the feel of her skin.

"Grandma?" he asks, with a little nervous tension in his voice.

Grandma Lee doesn't notice Steven's unusual behavior and she continues fixing his sandwich as she answers him calmly, "Yes?"

Steven continues to look at his grandmother in disbelief and it becomes clear that for some reason he's overwhelmed by the fact that she's alive. He hugs her and presses the side of his face into her side as he takes a deep breath and begins crying, "You're real... Grandma, you're alive, you're alive... you're really here and you're alive!"

With Steven hugging and weeping uncontrollably, Grandma Lee doesn't understand what's triggered this sudden surge of emotional outburst in Steven. She's uneasy with his repeating that she's alive, as if for some reason she shouldn't be. Still, she consoles him with a hug as she asks him, "What's the matter with you?... What's wrong?"

Then right in her arms, without any warning of any kind, as if the rapture just happened right then and there, Steven vanishes in her arms. No residual puff of smoke or flash of light. She was holding him in her arms. He was holding her tightly and crying, then he vanished. The sound of his voice was extinguished from the room with just the same sudden evacuation, not leaving an echo of sound nor a whisper of air in the room to express the slightest hint that he was ever there.

Resisting the instinct to scream and frightened by what just happened, Grandma Lee feels a cold chill move through the room like a wave and goose bumps tingle her starting at her right forearm and systematically working their way over her body. How is this possible? She wonders in horror. Did God just rapture her grandson and leave her behind? This can't be happening, she thinks to herself, Am I dreaming? The thought of being left behind to endure the tribulation trials and the of the mark of the beast, prophecies from the Bible awaken a new fear. One that until now she believed she would never have to concern herself with. She wonders to herself, how could this be. This can't be true.

Then the front door visible from where she's standing suddenly opens and startled by the unexpected intrusion, Grandma Lee gasps, "Oh my god!"

Amy walks in carrying a bag of prescription medicine, and another bag with a few household items, not hearing Grandma Lees gasp or noticing her despair, she complains about the customer service at the store.

"Sorry we took so long... they really should hire more people at that stupid store, their so darn slow..."

Then Amy notices the look of terror on Grandma Lee's face.

"Mom?... Are you OK?"

Grandma Lee braces herself on the kitchen counter top as if maintaining her balance and now her expression changes from terror to mixed fear and confusion as she watches Steven walk in the front door licking an ice cream cone and he immediately stops when he notices the cartoons playing on TV, and sits on the floor in the same exact place he was just moments ago. Amy hurries to Grandma Lee's side and when she realizes her distress has something to do with Steven her concern grows.

"Mom! What's the matter?!"

Still in shaking nervously, confused, in shock and speechless, Grandma Lee holds onto Amy who walks her to the nearest chair at the dining room table and sits down. With a terrified look, Grandma Lee still hasn't taken her eyes off of Steven who's in the living room watching Saturday morning cartoons playing on the TV.

Chapter 7

26 Years later.
April, 2010
Thursday, 3:40 p.m.

Now 34 years old, Steven has been married to Vicky, the woman he loves, and together they are the parents of two boys "Erick and Teddy." Amy is about 55 years old now and Grandma Lee died of natural causes about 10 years ago.

Steven is driving home from work, on the freeway in his work car, an old beat up Nissan two door sedan. The afternoon traffic is moving along slowly but as steady as usual for this time of day. The only reason they call it rush hour is probably because no matter how much of a rush your in it'll take you a minimum of an hour to get out it. Singing along quietly and drumming his fingers on the steering wheel with the Naked Eyes remake of Always Something There to Remind Me, playing loud on the radio, he's cut off in mid verse when his cell phone rings. He lowers the radio volume he answers the phone call with a finger tap on the hands free Bluetooth device held in his ear.

"Hello?"

Speaking in her most sexy voice on the other end of the call, Vicky asks him, "What are you wearing?"

Steven and Vicky occasionally tease each other, roll playing with playful banter occasionally when calling each other just to break the ice with a little humor. Once Vicky called pretending to be from the electric company telling him that their electric bill hadn't been paid for the past 3 months and this was just a courtesy call giving him one last chance to pay the bill of $800 before they turn the power off. Steven didn't recognize Vicky's voice and freaked, nearly running the car off the road. Of course Vicky chalked one up in her gotcha column. Since then Steven has programmed his phone ringer to let him know it's Vicky calling. Instantly he recognizes Vicky's ring tone and he plays along.

"Just sitting here in my tighty whiteys."

"Oooh, I bet you could use a nice hot bath and message," she replies.

"Oh yeah, baby... How'd you know I like my water hot?"

"Everybody likes it hot at first."

"Wait a minute, Vicky? Is that you?"

Breaking out of character, she says, "You know it's me, stupid."

"I know, I'm just kidding... What's up?"

"I'm just calling to see if you're off work yet. How your day's going... the usual stuff."

"Oh. Well in that case, I'm on my way home. And I'm having a great day, so far... How's yours?"

"Fine... Oh, by the way, Teddy needs some new sneakers. The ones he's wearing are starting to get holes in them."

"OK, no prob, can it wait till Saturday?"

"I guess it can. How far away are you?"

"I'm about 5 minutes away. You need me to pick something up?"

"No... I just wanted to say hi, and find out if you were on the way, so I could start making dinner. Oh, and let you know about Teddy's shoes."

"OK babe , I'll see you in a few. Bye jelly."

"Bye peanut butter."

Luke taps the button on the side of his ear piece to hang up the phone call and turns the radio volume back up as he continues his drive home.

*

Steven steers his car into the driveway and parks next to a small white, Ford Escape SUV; the family car, and the newer of the two cars he and Vicky own He prefers to thinks of the Ford as Vicky's car more than his, since she drives it about 80 percent of the time. It's the car they use when they go out together, as a family for dinner, shopping or wherever.

In the living room is 9 year old Teddy, sitting on the floor and his brother Eric sitting on the couch and is older than him by one year. The boys are operating wireless video game controllers, as they engage in combat with another team of commandos in a simulated urban warfare battlefield on their favorite video game. Steven walks through the front door carrying his lunch box and not missing a beat or taking their eyes off the TV; they both greet their dad.

"Dad!" Teddy says with an artificial hint of happiness in his voice.

"Hey Dad. How was work?" Erick says, in his

typical nonchalant casual tone.

"Hey you guys! Work was fine. How was your day?"

"Good," Erick answers.

Teddy answers, "Fine," and quickly adds, "I need new shoes, Dad."

"Yeah, Mom told me... We'll get them Saturday."

"Thanks Dad."

Steven makes his way to the kitchen, and as he cuts though the dining room he hears his cell phone ring. Looking at his caller ID and sees that it's his boss, John, and he stops to answer it. "Hello?"

"Hi Steve, it's me John."

"What's up John?"

"Steve we need you to take some time off."

It's not unusual in Steven's line of work to have to take a day off now and then due to job scheduling, bad weather, or any other unforeseen circumstances, but to get the call from John personally raises red flags.

"Why, what's wrong?" Steven asks.

"Nothings wrong, it's just that business is slow and we don't have enough projects going to keep everyone busy. You're low man on the totem pole chief."

"Am I being fired?"

"No, it's not like that at all. Trust me when things pick up, we'll call you back."

"How long?"

"Maybe a month or two... Let's see how things go."

Steven's heard this song and dance before. The last time Steven got laid off, it lasted more than four months, and he's been working for three months since then and now he gets this call. By all accounts this is bad news. Even with Vicky working part time, her pay and his unemployment check will just barely be enough to pay the bills and put food on the table. But as luck would have it, as with the last time he was laid off; food and bills are never the only expenses that happen. Unexpected circumstances such as a flat tire can easily be an $80 setback that would push the budget into the negative. Yes, this is bad news.

"Well, what can I say?" Steven says, "Don't forget me."

"We won't buddy."

"Alright, talk to you later."

Steven hangs up. Thinking about what just happened. Was it something I did or said? Did I just jinx myself earlier? Did I cause fate to make me lose my job just now, when I asked earlier, what could possibly go wrong? The questions run though his mind troubling him. This is bad news. On the job they had the saying, "No news is good news," meaning that if you never got any feedback, it meant you were doing alright. The downside to that philosophy was that if the boss wanted to talk to you it could only be bad news. Steven doesn't want to bring down Vicky and the boys with this bad news. Why ruin what has been such a good day? Well, like they say, no news is good news.

Walking into the kitchen, he kisses Vicky on the cheek and sets his lunch box on the floor next to the refrigerator. Vicky who is standing in front of the electric stove, stir frying the main course, which looks like a beef and broccoli stew, as a side of green vegetables simmer in another pan on one of the back burners.

Vicky, 33 years old, has been married to Steven

for 13 years now. Steven likes it when she ties her light brown hair back in a pony tail, a hair style she usually wears when she's in the kitchen making food or when she's doing housework. It reminds him of when he used to watch her play sports back in high school during PE. That's when she first caught his eye, out on the basketball court with the other girls, dribbling the ball and taking the shot. Even though they were all wearing the same gym clothes she stood out among them. The way she looked, the way she moved, the enthusiasm she had about the game. Basketball wasn't Steven's game, nor did he have any interest watching the pros play. But the first time he saw Vicky on the court, he found a game particularly more interesting and worth watching. It didn't mattered whether she scored or not. She was the winner in his eyes no matter what the score was. Just watching her do her part on the court and the enjoyment she got out of it, made it entertaining for him. Back then he just knew somehow, she was the one.

"Hi," he says as he looks over her shoulder down at what's cooking.

"Hi, honey," she says, and continues cooking.

As he watch her stirring the food in the frying pan, he decides to tell her about his not working tomorrow, but with a little spin on it.

"Well, I have some good news... I get to sleep in tomorrow."

"No work?" she asks.

Steven smiles, lifts his chin, puts his fists on his waist and juts his chest out as if he were a super hero of some sort. In this case, "Deception man."

"Three day weekend baby!" he says with a flare.

"For you maybe... I still have to go to work, and

the boys have school."

Vicky works part-time at Magnolia Elementary School. The same school Eric and Teddy attend, which makes taking them to and from school everyday more convenient.

"Well we still get to spend Saturday and Sunday together," Steven says.

Steven leaves the kitchen unbuttoning his shirt, preparing to take a shower. That was easy, he thinks. I just bought Friday, and the weekend won't need any explaining. But I'll probably have to explain Monday on Sunday. Oh well, I'll just worry about crossing that bridge when the time comes.

Chapter 8

**Friday,
2:30 a.m.**

In the middle of the night with all the lights off, the furniture and other details can still be made out thanks to the slightly illuminated window blinds lit up by the bright moonlit night. Not a hint of movement or a whisper of sound is evident throughout the non-bedroom portion of the house. Vicky doesn't remember what woke her up, only that since she was stirred from her sleep, she needed to make a bathroom run and after she dealt with natures calling, she was quietly walking back to the bedroom, when she noticed the light coming from the kitchen down the hall. There wasn't any light a minute ago when she first awoke. Maybe Steven is up for a cup of water, is her first thought. Then she notices he's still in bed when she returns to the room.

With Steven in bed, that most likely means it's one of the boys in the kitchen or someone just forgot to turn the light out. Vicky gets back out of bed and goes to take a look for herself, prepared to scold one or both of the boys for being up so late. As she makes her way down the hall, she hears what sounds like a spoon being dropped in a coffee cup. Then she hears a mans voice which causes her to stop dead in her tracks. She's unable to make out exactly what's being said, but he kind of sounds like Steven.

The thought of a stranger in the house, has her spooked to the point of not perusing this any further on her own. So she hurriedly returns to the bedroom to wake up Steven. When she gets back to the bedroom, and sees Steven in bed, it further removes any doubt that she may have been mistaken about seeing him in bed before. Even more worried now, she nervously shakes him trying to wake him up.

"Steven, wake up! Wake up! Someone's in the house!" She whispers intently.

Groggy and disoriented, Steven wakes up, 'Wha... what's the matter?"

"Shhh...There's someone out there...Listen...," Vicky says, silencing him.

Still rubbing his eyes and wondering what time it is, Steven sits listening quietly with Vicky, then they hear sounds of movement coming from the kitchen.

Vicky flinches and says, "See! Someone's out there!"

Frustrated from being awaken from his sleep, and not convinced that there's an intruder in the house Steven casually gets out of bed, but not without voicing his opinion, "Sounds like one of the boys is up for a midnight snack."

"No it's not the boys. That's what I thought first, so I started to go out there. Then I heard a man talking," Vicky says.

Vicky already wearing her robe follows Steven

out to the hall, who still not completely convinced it's not one of the boys. Immediately they can see that the kitchen light is on. But the voices have stopped. They quietly walk down the hall towards the kitchen.

When they get to the kitchen it is evident that whoever was in here Steven missed them by seconds. One of the cabinets is wide open, and a tea kettle is in the sink with the water running fast to fill it. The tea kettle is only about halfway full of water, so whoever placed it under the running faucet must have put it there less than half a minute ago, and is most likely still in the house or nearby.

Steven turns off the water, as Vicky makes her way to the boys bedroom. Then Steven hurriedly makes his way to the front door just to discover it locked from the inside. He rushes to the back door of the house only to find that it too is also locked from the inside. He checks the closets and the rest of the house where someone could possibly be hiding, but doesn't find anyone. Checking all the windows of the house, Steven doesn't find any proof of intrusion.

Vicky quietly opens the door to the boys bedroom and sees them both in there beds, sound asleep. Nothing about the way they are sleeping indicates that either of them have recently been out of bed. She goes to Erick and gently tries to wake him up, but he tiredly refuses. Then she tries the same with Teddy, and he too is sound asleep. Vicky comes out of the room, quietly closing the door behind her. And goes back to the kitchen.

Steven is standing in the middle of the kitchen contemplating possible explanations .

Vicky walks in quietly and notices the expression of confusion on Stevens face. Then Steven looks at Vicky and asks her, "Was it them?"

Vicky knows it wasn't the boys she heard, and finding them asleep in there room was no surprise to her. The reason she went to check on them was just to make sure they were alright.

"They're both asleep."

"Are you sure?" Steven asks.

"It wasn't them. They're both sound asleep. I'm telling you, Steven, I heard a man talking."

"What did he say?"

"I don't know. I didn't hear what he was saying. I heard his voice, he kind of sounded like you..,

"Me??"

"...but I knew it couldn't be, because you were still in bed. I got scared, so I went to get you."

"Vicky, I checked all the doors and windows. Everything's locked from the inside. The doors are dead bolted."

"What about the..."

"I checked all the closets and the bathrooms too. There's nobody else is in the house."

"Should we call the police?"

"What for? To tell them we think someone came in and tried to make a cup of coffee? Then changed their mind, let themselves out and locked the door behind them? Even if that's what really happened, I'm not sure what crime was committed. Nothings missing."

Steven and Vicky stand silent for a moment, thinking about what just happened.

Then Vicky says out loud what their both thinking, "You think maybe it was a ghost?"

Although Steven was thinking the same thing, he's not completely convinced that it wasn't the boys who just stirred up all this mayhem. To make light of it and try to bring down the anxiety that both he and

Vicky are feeling, he sarcastically says, "Right... we're being haunted by the coffee drinking ghost."

Not giving in to the humorous implication, Vicky's bothered by the invasion of their personal space, but worse then that, what they could be dealing with here is some uninvited supernatural entity that just made its presence known by physically moving things around in her kitchen. Vicky would prefer that Steven had found proof that someone had broke in and tried to rob them. The thought of a ghost haunting her house is by far more unsettling.

"It's not funny, Steven."

"Vicky, come on... Let's go back to bed, it's probably just one of the boys, sleepwalking. I'm sure we'll find out in the morning. It's late, the kids have school, you have to work..."

They both walk back to the bedroom turning out the lights behind them. Vicky still nervous about it stays close to Steven.

"Steven, it wasn't the boys... I'm telling you, I'm not crazy, I heard a man..."

Chapter 9

Steven is dreaming he is in the batting cages hitting pitches. Raziel is standing across from him watching. Wearing the same white dress, she doesn't show any sign of aging since the night they first time they met, 26 years ago. Steven's having a good time. He making perfect contact with a couple of pitches and sending the ball flying like a home run over the center field fence.

"You're pretty good at this," Raziel says.

"Thank you," Steven says, smiling.

Steven looks over at Raziel and notices she is glowing. He knows that she tends to glow when she's emotional or happy about something.

"That's so cool when you glow like that."

'You really like it?, Thank you." she says, as if she were a young lady who just had her hair styled or bought a new dress.

"It looks nice on you."

She smiles, and then stops as she looks around and her glow dims out.

"You know they closed this place down," she says.

Steven hits one more pitch and the pitching machine stops automatically shuts off.

"Really? When?" Steven asks.

Although the batting cages he's dreaming of are a real place from his memory his dreams have kept them unchanged in 26 years. He looks around and the place starts transforming right before his eyes. Cracks appearing in the concrete then weeds appearing in the cracks. On the structural housings of the pitching machines rust corrosion appears on the metal surfaces and the painted surfaces start to fade, then some of the paint flakes off.

"A couple of years ago. Doesn't quite look the same anymore, does it," Raziel says.

Steven looking around at the deterioration of the place feels a little sad about the way the place has gone down then he points to his head. As he says, "It still looks good up here."

With the mind power of control he has of this dream he instantly causes the place to be restored, and the place to new again.

"Nice," she says with a smile.

"I think it looks better this way."

Raziel and the batting cages fade away as Steven's dream changes and he now finds himself swimming in the ocean. Though he's un-phased by the drastic change in scenery he stops swimming and treads water. It's broad daylight and Steven squints from the bright sun shining down. Looking around in all directions till he notices a yacht with two people on board, anchored about 50 yards away, so he waves his arms trying to be seen. Then he yells, "Hey! Over here!... Ahoy!"

The two people don't notice him, so he just starts swimming towards the boat. He swims about 15 yards, when he feels something brush by him in the water. He starts to panic thinking it might be a shark. Then he sees a shark fin to his right, so he starts swimming as fast as he can towards the boat. As he swims he keeps getting bumped by the shark. Then he gets pulled under. As he sinks under the water being pulled down by his feet, he notices that he doesn't seem to be suffering from any lack of breath. It's as if he were able to breath under water somehow. Sinking into the depths of the ocean water, the vision of a Circle K store sign flashes in his mind. Then back in the ocean sinking still deeper. He see's newspapers scattered on a white tiled floor. Back to water sinking still. Then he see's himself as if he were on the outside looking in, someone with his back turned to him pointing a gun to his forehead and pulls the trigger.

Steven wakes up startled from his dream. He's home, dry and safe in bed. Looking at the clock radio on his nightstand he sees that it's 5:31 am.

Chapter 10

**Friday,
6:15 a.m.**

Steven is in the kitchen. Since he doesn't have to work today, he's wearing an old pair of gym shorts and a T-shirt. Though his dream earlier was nightmarish, he's in a good mood this morning and he's make the most of his day off so he's decided to help Vicky with some of the household chores. Right now since he's up early and hungry, he's making breakfast for everybody.

Vicky walks in checking text messages on her cell phone, and sees Steven at the kitchen stove.

"You're up early. I thought you were gonna sleep in," she says.

"Want an omelet?" He asks.

Vicky looks at the set up Steven has neatly laid out for making omelets. 4 bowls, one with scrambled eggs, one with cheese, one with chopped bell pepper and tomato, and one with chopped ham.

"Ooh, yes, that sounds good."

"What about the boy's? Do they'll want an omelet?"

"Erick does. Not Teddy, he prefers scrambled eggs."

Just then Erick walks in.

"It smells good in here," he says.

"Don't you mean good morning?" Vicky says, policing Eric on his manners.

"Oh yea, Good morning," he corrects himself.

"Good morning." Steven says.

"Dad's making bacon and omelets." Vicky says.

"Cool!" Eric cheers.

"Where's your brother, Teddy?" Vicky asks.

"He's looking for his Nintendo DS."

Vicky is all too familiar with the routine her boys go through in the morning and how easily distracted they get looking for anything else to do, other than getting ready for school in the morning. "He's not taking it to school. Go tell him he doesn't have time for that, and to come have some breakfast."

Erick goes back to the bedroom to find Teddy.

After Erick leaves the kitchen, Steven looks at Vicky who's now putting her cell phone in her purse and fumbling through the contents looking for something else. "So what do you think?" he asks.

"I haven't told them anything," she says, then she finds her keys and sets them down on an end table next to the couch in the living room near the front door and sets her purse next to them, then returns to the kitchen morning room and sits down at the table.

"Told us what?" Eric says as he enters the room and sits at the table.

Teddy's walks in right after him playing his handheld Nintendo game.

Steven says, "Morning, Teddy. Want an omelet?"

"Can I have scrambled instead?" he asks.

Proud of her prediction, Vicky says, "Told you."

"Told us what?" Eric asks again.

"Mom and I have something to ask you guys about last night," Steve says.

Teddy takes a seat at the table, still playing his video game.

"You know your not taking that to school, right?" Vicky tells Teddy.

"Yes... I know," he says.

"So put it away."

"Can I finish this level, first?" he pleads.

"You can finish the level after breakfast."

Steven, still cooking breakfast tries to lighten things up with a little humor. And chimes in, "When I was your age, we didn't have Nintendo. We had to finish the levels with our bare hands."

Teddy turns his game off and is a little frustrated because of it. Nor is he amused with his dads dry sense of humor at a time when he needs to be saving the Nintendo world from all the cyber bad guys. "That doesn't make any sense. If you didn't have Nintendo, how could you have any levels?" he says.

Steven just smiles and cuts to the chase finally, asking, "Hey guys. Did any of you get up in the middle of the night?"

"No," Teddy answers.

"No, why?" Erick asks.

"Nobody got up last night and turn on the kitchen lights, or turn on the water?"

Both boys shake their heads, and say no.

Trying to get the boys to reconsider their answers and understand that all he wants to do is solve the mystery, he says, "Look, nobody's in any trouble. Just tell us the truth. Last night, someone came to the kitchen and turned the lights and water on. And forgot to turn them both back off. Are you both sure it wasn't either of you?"

Erick speaks out on behalf of Teddy and himself, "We're not lying dad... Someone forgot to turn out the lights?"

Steven serves the breakfast plates and joins everyone at the table with a plate of his own.

Teddy confirms their plea again, "Dad, we're telling the truth. It wasn't us."

"I believe you," Steven says. Then adds, " But remember, God's always watching, and he knows everything."

They sit quiet for a moment and say a silent prayer giving thanks for their breakfast.

Then Teddy asks, "So who was it?"

"We don't know?" Steven says.

Erick makes a ghostly noise saying, "Oooooooooooh." and moving his hands mysteriously and Teddy laughs.

Vicky doesn't find Erick and Teddy making fun of what happened funny and snaps at the boys, "Cut it out! Erick, Teddy. Boys... eat you're breakfast."

Chapter 11

Later that morning.

In a different part of town, Joey Lester is sitting on the edge of the queen-size bed putting on a T-shirt. His girlfriend "Tina Brant" is still in bed, sleeping face down under the sheets. Tina works as a bartender on the closing shift at a small bar called "Lucy's" where she and Joey first met about a year ago. Joey works day shift at Wal-Mart and just like last night he often hangs out at Lucy's bar drinking late into the evening, often until closing time, about 2:00 in the morning.

Right now Joey's a little hung-over and knows he's running late for work. As he sits on the edge of the bed, in the one bedroom of their small apartment. He looks around the room searching for anything that might trigger his mind to come up with an excuse that he hasn't already used. Nothing comes to focus except the intermitted wave of pressure from his headache. Standing up, he reaches out for the wall to help him keep his balance. His equilibrium takes a second to settle as he holds his place and leans his head to the right slowly keeping in line with the room tilt caused by the dizziness he found himself in this morning under the influence drinking so much last night.

"Tina... Hey Tina!, Wake up... have you seen my keys?" he says with a bit of lazy slur in his voice.

"I don't know," she mumbles, her response borderline impossible to make out because she's still half asleep and doesn't want to be bothered.

Considering the possibility of using the lost keys as his excuse for being late sounds reasonable to Joey. That would make half the blame Tina's fault, he thinks to himself. Taking it to the next level, he could pass the blame as 99 percent her fault for being late to work. Makes perfect sense to him. If it's half her fault then she can't be angry at him since she's to blame equally. And at work since they think she's the one who's at fault then he doesn't deserve to be punished. Again he asks Tina about the keys.

"Tina I need my keys, so I can go to work."

She gets angry, because she knows what Joey's doing. He's pulled this stunt before. Last night she tried to tell him to stop drinking so much because he might have a difficult time waking up the next morning. He wouldn't have her telling him what he could or couldn't do. "Look I can stay up all night and still work the whole day tomorrow and not have any problems", he would say. As much as she wished he were right about what he was trying to prove, she knows now he woke up late and is just playing dumb and looking for an excuse for being late to work.

"I don't know, check the table?" she says.

Joey walks out to the kitchen and looks on the small square table against the wall. On it next to a couple of empty beer cans and an ash tray half full of cigarette butts, he sees the car keys on a ring with about 6 other keys.

Joey sits at the table and lifts the keys from the table with his finger through the key ring and twirls them as the gears in his head turn in search of a new excuse for being late to work. "I cant just go in and not say nothing. They'll definitely call me in the office for that. I need to call in right now with a reason to pacify the boss." He lights a cigarette and takes a deep inhale, holds it for a second and puffs it out straight up. "What am I doing?", he thinks to himself, "I'll just call and my survival instinct will kick in an excuse for me. Good old instinct... never failed me yet." He stops twirling the keys, opens his cell phone and makes the calls.

After a few rings a female voice at the other end of the line answers, "Wal-Mart."

"Hi, this is Joey let me speak with Mikey."

"Mikey the shift manager?"

"Yea, the manager Mikey."

"He's not in the office at the moment, can I take a message?"

"Look I need to talk to him now, it's very important."

"In that case I'll page him, and I'm going to put you on hold for a minute till he comes to the phone. Don't hang up, OK."

"I know, yea, that's OK, I'll wait."

Joey takes another puff from his cigarette. And starts grooming his hair with his hands as if Mikey could possibly see him through the phone. It doesn't take long before Mikey's voice comes on the phone and Joey's tone of voice gives evidence to the fact that he's speaking to someone more important. Joey has the phone pressed up against his ear so tight hoping

it will help wake up better and maybe Mikey won't
able to hear any slur or evidence that he just woke
up less than ten minutes ago.

"Hey... Mikey, it's me Joey..."

"Are you calling in sick?"

"No, I'm not calling in sick..."

"What's up, then? Why are you calling?"

" Look, I went to my car this morning and I had a
flat tire, so I had to change it. I would have been
there on time but the lug bolts were on so tight, I had
to search the garage and the whole house for a
breaker bar. And..."

"And what? Go on."

"Well... long story short... I'm running a little
late..."

"Really..."

"Really Bro, I'm not lying... I'm putting the jack
away and I realized I it took me so long to break the
lugs loose, I'd better call you and tell you I'm running
late..."

"Alright, well take care of what you need to do.
We'll see you when you get here."

"OK, thanks, I'll be there in about 15 minutes...."

"Oh and hey, don't speed or run any stop signs.
We don't want you to be any later than you already
are, OK."

"OK, bye."

Joey slaps shut his flip phone and sits for a
moment twirling the keys again. He takes a puff from
his cigarette proud of his God given gift of gab. His
remarkable ability to talk his way through any
situation under pressure and sometimes without a
moments notice. Standing up he stretches and
yawns, then he casually strolls out the door. "Good
old instinct."

Chapter 12

Later still that morning.

Steven is jogging on the sidewalk towards his home, wearing the same gym shorts and T-shirt he was wearing at breakfast which are now half drenched with sweat. He is little out of shape and out of breath due to the lack of regular exercise and the excessive junk food eating habit he developed during the past year.

The sweat soaked patches on his shirt absorb the coolness of the mild morning breeze delivering a welcomed relief from heat of the sun radiating down on him, and what heat doesn't directly hit him from above reflects back up off the sidewalk.

Reaching the front porch of his house he walks to the shade and catches his breath as he stands hunched with his hands braced on his knees like an infielder in a baseball game waiting for the batter to hit the next pitch. After his heart rate slows and his breathing is relaxed he takes a seat on the porch bench to cool off before going inside. Sitting there relaxing, he looks out at the neighborhood, and reflects back to a time when he was much younger, about 9 years old. He remembers how he used to play hide and seek with the other kids in his grandmas neighborhood. Looking at a tree in the middle of the yard it leads him to remember back to one specific day .

*

"5,10,15,20...," Cindy count leaning into the tree with her arms folded across her eyes which are closed tight.

Steven and his other friends are running off in different directions in search of hiding places.

"...35,40,45,50..."

Steven runs past the hedge of his grandma's front yard and stops at Lisa's front yard, looks to his left then runs towards the area where the hedge meets the fence to his grandmas backyard.

"...75,80,85,90,95,100. Apples, peaches, pumpkin pie, who's not ready holler aye!" Cindy hollers.

Steven's waits crouched down behind the hedge. Then he looks through the chain link fence that separates the front and back yard. He sees the man wearing the blue shirt and black pants with his back turned to him standing in his grandma's back yard. He can't see the face of the man who seems to be talking quietly to himself. Then he sees Skipper, come around the corner from behind the house. The fact that Skippers leash is missing from his collar comes to mind again. He remembers how the leash hook was stuck to the collar and he tried and tried to get it to come loose but with no success. Yet here is Skipper still wearing his collar and no leash. Did the man in the backyard take the leash off. And if he did, why. We never did find that leash. Skipper trots towards the man and just before he reaches him, he stops, sits and looks up at the position next to him. Focusing on the position next to the man, where Skipper is looking, the image of the ghost woman in white clothes begins to take shape. Although she is transparent he can see her beautiful face clearly.

Steven focuses now his memory of what she looked like and it strikes him as odd that even though he's never seen this ghost woman again or even thought about this day for 26 years, he still hasn't forgotten what she looks like. 26 years older he sees the beautiful ghost woman and as attractive as she is, something about her causes him to feel close to her. As if she were the ghost of a relative from his past or something. The feeling he gets inside prevents him from feeling any sexual attraction, and at the same time wins his trust without merit. Looking directly at her and she at him, he sees her lips moving. She's saying something. He's unable to make out what it is she's saying. Then it becomes evident that she's not talking to him but instead to the man next to her, because he reacts by turning around and looks directly at Steven. Steven catches a glimpse of his face just as he makes eye contact and the man disappears.

Steven stands up in a state of shock. He thought that being an adult now, his reaction to seeing the two ghost disappear wouldn't have the same sinister effect it had on him back then, but the shock is just as intense if not more now. And this time for reasons entirely different from what he was thinking 26 years ago. This time the man he remembers seeing is no stranger to him. Not having ever thought about this day again the years past without him ever learning what any of this meant or who the man was. He never knew till now that the man he saw that day was himself.

Skipper gets up like nothing unusual has just happened, and trots to the back behind the house.

Having given away his position Cindy spots him and runs up to tag him and starts yelling, "I got you Steven!... Steven's it!, Steven's it!"

*

Steven's never thought about this event again till now. And now he realizes the man he was looking at back then wasn't just a dead ringer for himself. It was himself. "But how could I possibly see my future self... How is that possible?", he thinks "If it was me, does this mean I died in the near future soon my ghost will haunt my past. Seeing myself in my past is something that's already happened. There's no question about that. It already happened. What I don't understand is, why would I haunt the past the way I did? The me that I saw back then looked the same age I am now. Not older. So does this mean that some time soon I might die?"

Steven snaps out of the thoughts that are going through his mind, and wonders to himself, "Why am I thinking of this now? All these years go by and after the night it happened, I never gave it another thought. Why would this suppressed memory suddenly wake itself up and make itself known now?"

Just then from the corner of his eye, through the

window of his house, he sees the figure of a man
inside the house moving through the living room.

Steven jumps up quickly from the bench and
runs to the front door. Taking out his key he
nervously struggles to slip it into the keyhole. He
turns the key, unlocking the door and he tries to
push it open, but the door only opens about 3 inches
before it is met with a force from the other side. The
intruder seems to be blocking the door from the
inside. With the door jammed open about 3 inches
Steven slightly backs off on the pressure he's
applying towards opening it. Then the door pushes
back as if to shut on him, but he catches it in time
and doesn't let it close. It's clear now that the
intruder is on the other side of the door, and whoever
it is, he's preventing Steven from entering. Now
Steven is pushing as hard as he can and feels that
he's slowly winning the battle.

Steven shouts, "Whoever you are, you're
busted!!... You're not getting away man!!!"

Then for no reason, the pressure on the other
side of the door is released. And the door swings wide
open. And as fast as the door opens Steven rushes
into the entry way almost stumbling to the ground
but instead retains his balance. Steven looks left and
right, then behind the door quickly only to find
nobody there. There's no way somebody could have
released the door and ran off without being seen by
him. But someone was there on the other side of the
door. He saw the man through the window. Steven
runs through the house using his peripheral vision to
scan left and right till he reaches the back door in the
kitchen only to see it dead bolted locked from the
inside. Then he rushes frantically through the rest of
the house searching under beds, in closets and

behind doors for the intruder. But not a hint of a break in or in this case, a break out can be found. And just like last night, all the doors and windows are locked from the inside.

Steven returns to the living room where he saw the intruder through the window. He stands at the spot in between the TV and the couch where he saw him. Waiting nervously for something to happen he takes a deep breath and holds it and lets it out as quietly as he can as he listens in total silence, looking around the room not seeing anyone or anything moving. Nothing except a spot on the living room couch that appears to be slowly returning to shape as if someone had been from sitting there a short time ago. He looks at his hand and observes a slight nervous shaking.

The ghost in his house has just made his next move. Steven doesn't want to believe this is happening in his home, but he can't deny what he just saw. He's pretty sure he saw the man in his peripheral vision. And the shoving match at the front door couldn't have been just the wind or a jammed door. It pushed back on him with the equal strength to his own. Still..., not finding anyone in the house gave Steven a thread of doubt to string together a theory that maybe nobody was ever here, maybe just saw a shadow or a reflection of something else and the front door was maybe just jammed when he tried to open it. But when he saw the depression on the couch slowly disappearing he had to admit he felt a strange tingle flow through him. The last time he remembers feeling like this was that day he was just thinking of as he sat out on the front porch. That was the day 26 years ago in his grandmas front yard.

Chapter 13

In the games and puzzles section of the toy department in Wal-Mart, Joey is working his normal shift stocking shelves. He started working for the store about 3 months ago when his friend Tim cut him to the front of the line getting his foot through the door with the advantage of his own endorsement and got him hired on the midnight shift cleaning floors and bathrooms, and stocking shelves to start. Shortly after that Tim made it possible for him to secure a position on the dayshift in store by alerting him to apply for an opening before it was advertised. He helped him doctor his application with a little fudging of the numbers, some bogus past experiences, and again with the same insider endorsement. Since then, Tim has assured Joey that he needs to prove himself worthy by responsibly performing his duties, and showing up regularly and on time.

Lately Steven's been testing the waters by taking extended breaks and showing up late for work and budding up to his supervisor Mikey, and laughing off occasional advice from up the chain. Right now he's talking on the phone with Tina and is trying to convince her that he deserves free drinks at Lucy's bar while he waits for her shift to end.

"That's great, tell them you can close the place down by yourself and I'll be there waiting for you to clock out, so the place will be safe. I'm like a bouncer for the place and they have me for free. I deserve a few free drinks just for my trouble, right?"

"I can't do that ,Joey. They'll never go for that."

"Why not?"

"First off, the place has never had any trouble in over ten years."

"Then maybe their due."

"Forget about it. I'm telling you they won't go for it."

"Then you should just spot me some drinks for free. You know... under the table."

"Are you crazy? If I get caught doing that, they'll fire me on the spot!"

"They won't find out. When it gets late, it's mostly just me and my homies that are there. They won't tell anybody."

"Joey, I can't tell you anything, without you trying to make it into a scam... I'm not gonna..."

Getting angry, Joey cuts her off, "Whatever, look, all I'm trying to do is make things better for us. We deserve a better life. And sometimes you just have to take what's yours..."

Just then the manger "Mikey" is walking by and he hears Joey talking on the phone. He stops at the end of the aisle and looks and sees Joey with one hand on his phone to his ear and the other shaking a Yahtzee box in the air. He walks toward Joey. And Joey sees him coming.

"Oh, crap. Here comes my boss, I gotta go," he tells Tina and slaps his phone shut, shoves it in his pocket and sets the Yahtzee box up on the shelf, and looks for the next item he needs to shelf in the shopping cart by him.

Shaking his head, Mikey approaches Joey and tells him, "Joey, Joey. You know the rules..."

"What, Mike? I'm working," Joey says defensively.

Mikey likes to believe he's a fair boss to his workers and has a clear understanding with all of his employees that he doesn't expect anything more than a fair days work for a fair days pay. Being a good friend of one of a manager from another department doesn't give him a green light to break the rules and Joey's been bending the rules and testing the limits as if he believes he was so valuable to the store, he's untouchable.

"Joey, you need to make your phone calls on your break, unless it's an emergency call. OK?"

"Well that's kind of what it was, Mikey. My girlfriend's grandma died, and she's kind of depressed.

"Oh. Well I'm sorry to hear that. Do you need some time off to go be with her?"

Joey knows he just dished out a load of bull to Mikey, and has no intention of losing a days pay just to make his lie look more real.

"Oh, no... It's not that bad... She'll be fine. We can talk when I get home."

"Well, look, if you need to go home and console your girlfriend for her loss, I totally understand. I just need you to remember, no phone calls here at work. If you need to make a call I would appreciate it if you would let me or one of the floor managers know or if it can wait just take it outside during your break. It won't be any big deal if you take care of it the right way. OK?"

Mikey walks away and Joey continues with his shelf stocking duties. After Mikey reaches the end of the aisle and turns out of sight, Joey pulls his phone from his pocket and checks it for messages.

Chapter 14

After his encounter with the unexpected ghost, Steven did one more sweep of the house, locked the front door, took a shower, got dressed and made good on his personal commitment to help Vicky with the house chores. He washed the dishes and pans from the breakfast he made earlier, made the beds in the master bedroom and the twin beds in the boys bedroom, picked up their dirty laundry off the floor, took a broom to the living room, dining room and kitchen floor as well as the halls in between, and emptied out all the full trash cans from the bathrooms to the kitchen. Doing the chores caused him to work up a sweat so he had to shower again and change into clean clothes.

Now with the chores completed Steven sits at the dining room table working on updating the resume he originally made a couple of years ago when he was out of work before. With papers scattered all over the table and the laptop propped open in front of him and the fact that he's only worked for one employer since the last time he was laid off, it doesn't take much effort to update his work history.

Still irritated about what happened earlier with the ghost intruder, he's wondering if he should tell anything to Vicky or the boys, who just happen to be pulling up on the driveway this very minute. The pushing match he had at the front door wasn't inconsequential by any means, but discovering that his opponent was an entity of an unknown origin combined with the mystery of the lights and the water being turned on last night, makes it difficult to dispute that what's happened within the past 14 hours is ominous at the very least. Had he simply seen a shadow of the ghost or heard movement in the house, he might've been able to explain it away. What ever it is that's haunting this house has made it known that it doesn't prefer the day shift or the night shift. It really hasn't made any attempt to communicate with us. Yet it hasn't wasted any time demonstrating it possesses power to move objects such as turning on the water or pushing on a door and preventing it from being opened. What does it want? Why has it chosen this home? (Vicky and the boys walk through the front door.) And what will it do if it gets angry? Thank God it hasn't made any attempt to connect with the boys.

Vicky comes into the dining room and the boys go to their room to put up their back pack and sweaters. "Hi, honey. How was your day off?" she asks Steven then kisses him on the cheek.

"Oh, fine, Steven says, "I went jogging after you guys left this morning. Boy am I out of shape. I don't like feeling this way."

Stevens loose fitting clothes hide the fact that

he's put on a few pounds, but his lack of vigor and the soreness in his muscles can't be hidden by loose fitting attire. Once in the past he went on a vegetarian diet for about two weeks to lose weight and it worked good for him, but immediately after he reached his goal he returned to eating the way he was before, and slowly began storing the extra calories, putting him back over the top.

"Are you going on a diet, again?" Vicky asks him.

"I might have to," Steven says, "Don't want to. But then whoever does. I really need to lose a few pounds."

"You're. not overweight," Vicky tells him, "I like the love handles. Something to hold onto."

"Well I don't like it. I feel like I'm overweight. In fact I know I'm definitely unfit. Maybe I just need to exercise."

Vicky notices all the papers scattered on the table.

"Whatcha got going on there?" she asks.

"Ah just putting together a back up plan for work. Just in case. You never know."

"Why, did you get fired today?"

"Of coarse not. Why would you say such a thing?"

"I'm just kidding with you, you Bozo. I know they wouldn't fire you. You're the best thing they got going for them. So, how'd it go here today? Was it all quiet? I see you did a lot of cleaning."

"It was OK today. Thanks for noticing."

"You do such a good job cleaning. You should do it all the time."

"I don't think so."

"So, did you see any ghost?"

Steven sits staring at the laptop for a couple of

seconds thinking then says, "You know… now that you mention it…"

Vicky's demeanor instantly switches from the happy go lucky, everything's fine and dandy, to the deer in the headlights, no way, OMG, as she takes a seat and leans in more attentively .

"No… You're lying… Really?" she asks, still not sure whether she should believe him or not.

"I'm not really sure what I saw."

"What do you mean? What did you see?"

"Well, when I got back from my run, I thought I saw someone in the house. Trough the window."

"A man?"

"Yea, no. I'm not sure. It kind of looked like a man. I just thought saw someone moving through the living room."

"Where were you at?"

"I was out on the front porch cooling off."

"Cooling off?"

"I told you, I just got back from my run."

"So what did you do?"

"Well that's the scary part," he tells her, "When I tried to open the door, it felt like he was inside trying to stop me from getting in the house, as if he was pushing it closed from the inside."

Vicky feels a chill creep up her spine as Steven tells her about the shoving match between himself and the ghost.

"Then it just stopped."

"What do you mean…it stopped?" Vicky asks with a nervous tension in her voice.

"The door swung open, and no one was there," he says, "There was no way someone could've let go of the door and run away without me seeing them. And yet there was no one in sight. I checked the rest of the house. It kind of reminded me of what happened last night."

Vicky holds herself as if to keep warm from the chill she feels creeping her.

"The doors and windows were locked from the inside, and there wasn't anyone here but me."

"I'm calling the pastor!" Having a deep fear that no good could possibly come from haunting spirits, Vicky feels spiritual entities shouldn't be challenged by anyone but men of the cloth. Even if the intentions of the person encountering the spirit were good, an encounter with an evil spirit would always yield negative results. Her biggest concern is that if they are evil spirits they could possibly try and possess someone in the home like in one of those demon possession movies. Definitely not a scene she wants occurring anywhere in her home.

"No! Vicky, you don't need to do that," Steven says, as he closes the laptop, stands up gathers the scattered papers and starts placing them in a folder.

"Steven, something seriously bad could be happening here. What if it's evil spirits?"

"We don't know if it's ghosts or evil spirits happening, or whatever."

Steven is being disingenuous, knowing how much he agrees with Vicky, but a part of him is harboring sentiments that prevent him from allowing his fear and concern let him believe that this could get out of control. Inexplicable as the last two encounters were he still senses that what is haunting his home are not evil spirits.

"Then what do you think it is?..." Vicky says, "Steven, something's haunting this place. And I'm not just going to stand by and do nothing..."

"Look, I just don't see a need to bother the

pastor right now. We really don't know for sure what's happening," Steven says, trying to convince her before she goes behind his back and makes an appointment with the pastor. The last time they had a visit with the pastor it almost turned into a marriage counseling session. Not that, that would be a bad thing for one to go through. All marriages have their rough times. But Steven feels his marriage isn't hurting for repair. And he's worried the pastor might just say the spirits are haunting their home because they have marital problems.

"I don't like it, What if this ghost or whatever this is, goes crazy and hurts one of the boys?"

"The truth is, neither you or I have actually seen any ghost," Steven reminds her, "The boys say they haven't seen or heard anything. But I'll tell you what. If it even looks like you or the boys are gonna get hurt, we'll get out of this house, call the pastor and have him pray away the evil spirits or whatever it is. We'll move if we have to. I promise. Just do me a favor, and don't call anyone yet. And don't say anything to the boys, OK. I don't want them getting spooked and being afraid to sleep in their room at night."

"They won't be afraid to sleep at night. Unless they start seeing things moving."

"Well I don't want to give them any reason to start looking for crazy things to happen."

"Like you did today?"

"I wasn't looking for something to happen, it just did... Can you hear how crazy this all sounds? I don't want the boys to start thinking their dad's losing his marbles or anything."

"You're not losing your marbles," Vicky says, "However...You did say you saw someone in the house."

"I said I thought I saw someone moving in the house... Maybe I shouldn't have told you."

"What do you mean by that?" Vicky asks, defensively.

"I didn't think you would make such a big deal of it," Steven says.

"You can't be too careful about these things, Steven."

"Alright already, let's talk about something else. What's the plan for dinner?"

"I haven't made any plans... It's Friday... can we order out?" Vicky asks.

"Pizza?" Steven suggest.

"Bambino's."

Vicky smiles.

"The boys will love that."

Chapter 15

**Saturday,
1:45 a.m.**

Located near the east end of the towns
business district is a small family owned bar and
grill, called "Lucy's". The owner, Lucy Handler
inherited it from her grandfather who named it after
his wife, her grandmother. When she retired, she
passed the business on to her two daughters who
shared responsibility managing, bartending and
working in the kitchen to learn the ropes then
gradually delegate as much of the duties as they
could allowing the business become self propelled.
The small business has been in the family as long as
the sisters could remember. Perhaps the best thing
Lucy's had going for it has been the steady flow of
regulars who have made this place part of their
nightly ritual, coming in for dinner every other night
or coming out for drinks and socializing and often
bringing with them a friend or two.

Tina applied for the position of assistant
bartender a year ago and even though she had no
experience at the time, she lucked out because the

current bartender enlisted in the military and was preparing to ship out for basic training. Her timing couldn't have been better. Instead of assistant, she was trained as his replacement on the closing shift.

Joey happened to come in with some friends late one Friday night and he and Tina hit it off immediately. He continued coming in every night after that for a week until she finally gave in and dated him. Shortly after that he convinced her to let him move out of his parents house and in with her.

Right now Tina is topping off a mug with beer from the tap. After tilting the mug so that the excess foam drips away she serves it to Joey, who's sitting at the bar next to his buddy Jeff. They're watching a basketball game with the volume muted on a TV mounted high on a wall decorated with NASCAR posters and mirrors framed with beer logos over shelves stacked of empty glasses and bottles of hard liquor behind the bar. One of the basketball players on the TV scores a basket.

Joey shouts a cheer of approval, "Yes! That's what I'm talking about!"

Jeff claps his hands and joins the rant, "Right on! Now just hang on to the 10 point lead for 2 more minutes and it's over baby!"

Tina still waiting across from Joey to pay for the beer she just served, says, "Two fifty for the beer, Joey."

"Put it on my tab."

"Joey, come on. You don't have a tab."

"Tina, don't embarrass me in front of my friend, I don't wanna have to go back there and slap you around, eh... Forget about it." Joey says, trying to give off a tougher than nails impression he learned from watching the movie "Donny Brasco."

Tina rolls her eyes and walks back to the register and pays for Joeys drink from her own pocket. A beer commercial comes on the TV, it's the one about the worlds most interesting man. Joey and Jeff stare lazily at the commercial even though they've already seen it about fifty times before.

"You know if he didn't have a ton of money, he wouldn't be interesting at all. He'd just be another drunk sitting right here with us," Jeff says.

Laughing at the concept of what Jeff just insinuated, Joey adds, "That's assuming he's interesting enough for us to even let him sit here with us."

"What a jerk," Jeff says with a small fit of anger, "I hate rich people."

Joey quickly adds, "I agree, it's them that are what's wrong with the world. Damn rich people think they own the whole world and we're supposed to all just suck up to them... take a number, get in line and wait our turn to kiss there..."

"Last call!!" Tina calls out as she flickers the house lights even though Joey and Jeff are the only two customers in the bar.

They sit quietly watching the TV for a moment just drinking and looking at the collection of fancy bottles of alcohol on the shelves behind the bar. Then Jeff breaks the silence.

"I wish I were rich," he says.

Joey adds, "Me too!"

Jeff raises his beer to make a toast.

Jeff says, "Here, here...To being rich one day!"

Joey raises his beer.

"I'll drink to that...We're gonna be rich!"

"Hey Tina!, We're gonna be rich!"

They both laugh.

Chapter 16

At precisely the same time that Joey and Jeff are toasting, Steven and Vicky are home on the other side of town in bed asleep. Steven starts to dream.

In his dream it's daytime and he's out in the neighborhood jogging. He's feeling the strain from the extra weight on body. Looking down at his own body he notices that he's about 25 pounds heavier than he was the last time he ran. He's wearing a short sleeve brown T-shirt and tight black shorts. He's struggling with his run but even as difficult time as he's having right now he's not giving up.

"Hang in there buddy!" Another runner says as he passes by him from behind. Steven notices that the other runner is wearing dark blue baggy running shorts and a gray T-shirt. Steven thinks to himself, this guy kind of looks like me but not as fat. He tries his best to catch him. The other runner is making good time and Steven struggles keep up.

Then he notices the other runner has stopped up

ahead at a red light. This is Steven's chance...but the closer he gets to this other man, the harder it is for Steven to move his legs. His legs begin to feel as if a magnetic force pulling them together, slowing him to a point where he can barely move at a walking pace.

Steven is just a couple of feet away and he hears a crow caw and he looks across the street and sees a large crow perched on a tall street lamp. Then he hears a car at the opposite corner screech to a halt almost hitting a bicycler who cut it off. The driver shouts out at the bicycler, "What's the matter with you!"

Steven keeps struggling to make progress toward the other runner. The man reminds him somehow of the ghost he thought he saw inside his house and he feels he need to make contact with him and get some questions answered. He continues until he's close enough to the other runner and reaches out to him, touches the mans shoulder and at the same time calls to him.

"Hey!"

The other runner turns around and disappears right before his eyes as does his entire surrounding, which is instantly changed into the interior of a silver car parked on a busy street in town. He's now wearing a long sleeve dress shirt and dark pants. Looking out the front window he notices it's night time now. Looking around at the inside of the car, he realizes he doesn't recognize this car. It's a BMW, judging by the familiar logo on the axis of the steering wheel. He see that the keys are still in the ignition. Forgetting that this is a dream he wonders to himself, "What am I doing here?"

Then he sees two thugs sitting on the curb with their hands cuffed behind their backs, which prompts him to look through the back window where he sees two plainclothes cops and a uniformed cop standing next to a patrol car with drugs on the hood. They seem to be busy discussing something with each other then one of them notices Steven in the car. "Hey, what the...!!!" he shouts.

Steven doesn't know what he's doing here or why, but it seems evident that he's not considered to be one of the good guys here. And these guys don't look like they're gonna believe he's not with the two thugs handcuffed on the ground. He thinks to himself, "I need to get out of here," and he starts the car up and shifts it into drive and screeches away. Hearing one of the cops hollering, "The car!!" While another hollers a hand held radio, "Garner, Garner you need to get back..."

He had no choice. It was his only chance of escape. The police would've never bought a story that he wasn't with the drug dealers. Not with him sitting right here in the front seat of their car.

The patrol man and one of the plainclothes cops jump into a patrol car and flip on the switch that turns on siren as they chase after Steven in the stolen BMW.

Steven speeds the car past traffic, splitting lanes, for about six blocks before he has to slow down at a red light that has too much cross traffic for him to cut through. He pulls up right next a familiar looking white Ford Escape SUV. Glancing to his right he immediately recognizes it. In the driver seat of the other car he sees himself. He also sees Vicky in the front passenger seat, and the boys in the back. Wondering for a micro second if that's himself in the other car, then who am I in this car? He looks quickly in the mirror and sees his own reflection. Then he looks back his other self in the other car. His other self doesn't see him in the BMW because he's looking in his rear view mirror to see what the commotion is with the police car with the siren wailing about three blocks back. Steven does however, notice that he has Teddy's attention from the back seat of the car .Teddy is looking directly at Steven with a puzzled expression on his face. Steven turns the steering wheel right and floors the accelerator driving the BMW into the intersection cutting off the white SUV and cutting into cross traffic going right.

About a block back the patrol car also turns right. Steven races a couple of blocks south seeing the patrol car a block away to his right, then he turns left and once again floors it and drives as fast as he can and passes another patrol car coming in the opposite direction. At this point he notices Raziel the angel in the back seat. Which makes him realize that this is a dream.

"Raziel! Why am I here? What's happening?" he shouts to her.

"Steven you're dream traveling!" she says.

"What!?"

"I said you're dream traveling!"

"What does that even mean!?"

"It means that your dreams are taking you to..."

"Forget about it, just help me get out of here!!"

"Right. Keep going straight about 4 blocks then turn right!"

"What will that do?!"

"That should get you to a wide open highway!"

"No!" he says, "What did you say? This is too real! I want to wake up! Just get me out of here!"

Steven continues swerving left and right avoiding collision with other traffic, sign posts, fire hydrants, and mailboxes by inches. "This car handles like a dream," he thinks, "Too bad it's just a dream, this car rocks."

Raziel knows that this dream Steven is in is taking place in his world now. Her mission to help him understand his dreams has just become complicated.

"This is real Steven!!"

"What?!" he asks, frantically.

"Your turns coming up!"

Steven cuts a hard right side swiping a parked car and immediately sees the freeway on ramp and he takes it cutting off another car that blows it's horn at him.

"Raziel!!" Steven shouts, "What do you mean?! Real?!"

There are now 4 police cars chasing Steven on the freeway. Steven is still driving as fast as the car can go to try and escape from the police. Everything gets lit up and now he sees that there's a helicopter flying high overhead with a high power spotlight shining down on him. He's still not sure what Raziel means by real. But if it means what he thinks it means, then he desperately needs to keep the police from getting close enough to identify him.

Slapping himself in the face, Steven tries to make himself wake up. But he doesn't feel any of the slapping which also doesn't have any effect on him. He hears the loud smack of his hand hitting his face but as if he were numb he feels the touch of his hand on his face but not the sting of the blows.

"Come on! Come on!! What's the matter with me!!" he shouts.

"Steven, If you woke up right now who would drive this car?" Raziel asks him.

"Nobody!!" Steven shouts, "It'll probably just crash! What's the big deal!? "

Steven notices the cars he's passing on the highway, semi truck, channel 3 news van, red 4 door sedan, then time slows down for him, or maybe his metabolism speeds up, either way the world around him has slowed to a snails pace and he sees two small children in the back seat of the sedan he passes. The two children are of no significance to Steven, other than the fact that if this car were to crash, it might involve the sedan in the next lane. Time returns to normal speed. Raziel sees that Steven now understands why he cannot just vanish from the fast moving vehicle in heavy traffic.

"Now you see why?" she asks.

"Yes! I get it," he says, "I can't just let this car crash... innocent people could get hurt... I gotta get off this freeway."

Steven sees an exit sign "Theodore Ave exit ¾ mile." A remote road near the outskirts of town. Perfect.

He maneuvers the car all the way to the left in the fast lane... and the police follow his lead. Then at the last possible second Steven pulls the car hard to the right cutting off the two right lanes and causes traffic to come to a screeching halt. He pulls into the Theodore Ave off ramp, slowing down enough to make a right turn then he floors it again and in no time it becomes evident that this off ramp is an "S" turn and he has to hit the breaks to make another left and a quick right then he floors the accelerator.

The bright wide spotlight shining down from the helicopter lit up the rural road making instant daylight where it shined and made visible the details. For the first ¼ mile there seems to be houses on the left side and some kind of warehouse on the right side. The entire stretch of two lane road seems to be lined with telephone poles. At first it seems the poles are on both sides then they only line the right side. Next to the line of telephone poles is a jagged ditch which appears to be about two to three feet wide and about three feet deep. No car would be able to get across it no matter how fast it were moving. Once past the two or three scattered houses, the sides of the road opened wide to dirt fields on both sides about half a mile from the freeway, Steven continued speeding the car as fast as it would go and he began to notice that the road was leading straight to a single mountain silhouetted on the dim horizon. Then off to the right side he sees two sets of red and blue flashing lights moving fast to intercept him at the end of the road he's speeding on. The two squad cars reach the intercept point before Steven does and make the turn and are now heading directly at him with their headlights on high beam shining right in his eyes. Steven cuts the wheels slightly to the left and slams the breaks at the same time bringing the car to a stop in the middle of the road. He shifts it into park leaving the engine idling as the two squad cars come to a stop about 50 feet up the road, they get out and take position behind their open doors with their guns drawn. With the spot light still beaming down, the helicopter circles high overhead.

Steven looks out his window and sees the patrol cars that were following him on the freeway approaching. Raziel is not with him anymore. Steven sits still with his hands on the wheel, not yet sure what it is he needs to do. He's innocent of having anything to do with the men they had in cuffs sitting on the curb back in town, but that doesn't excuse him from interfering with police business or leading them on this high speed chase. His only chance is to wake up before they see his face.

The patrol cars arrive all skidding to a stop and positioned to box him in from both sides of the road. All the police officers are now out of their cars taking cover behind them, drawing their weapons and aiming them at the stopped BMW. One of the officers dressed in street clothes, stops at the rear of the BMW. Two other cops are at the driver side front taking cover behind their patrol car. And another from behind, is making his way to the passenger side, all of them keeping a cautious distance. They can see the silhouette of the driver sitting in the driver seat of the BMW and even though they have their spotlights lighting up the car from both sides they're unable to make out the details of the drivers face on account of the backwash of light coming from the squad cars on both sides.

The news van pulls up behind the police cars and the crew jumps out and takes cover behind one of the patrol cars, camera rolling. And they too see the man in the driver seat, but even with the spot light from the helicopter shining down and the spot light from the patrol car shining right at him they're too are unable to make out what he looks like due to the backwash of light coming from the opposite side.

The plain clothes cop covers the driver side of the BMW from behind, angrily calls out to Steven.

"Driver show your hands!" he shouts.

Steven looks out the window then decides to duck down as low as he can in the front seat and covers his face repeating over and over to himself, "Wake up... wake up... wake up."

They all wait at a safe distance with their

weapons aimed through the windows of the idling car.

"Driver! Put your hands up where we can see them!" he shouts again.

The sound of the helicopter circling overhead fades away and Steven removes his hands from his face and finds himself in total darkness and he feels himself falling downward into the dark hollows. He looks down in the direction he's falling and sees no end in sight. As if he were dreaming a dream within his dream he sees himself kneeling on the ground holding his stomach. Then he sees himself remove his hands from his stomach and looking down his hands are stained with blood.

Then his hands are clean as he snaps out of the vision and finds himself on his knees on the ground in the batters box at the batting cages looking at his hands. Raziel is standing across from him. "Are you OK?" she asks.

Steven looks up at her and looking around he sees that he's at the batting cages, it's night. It's quiet. Calm.

"It all seemed so real" , he says, "Wait a minute, you said it was real. But how can it be real if it were a dream? I don't understand. What if the police had caught me and made an arrest. Or what if they didn't catch me but had seen what I look like? Then I would be wanted by the police. Raziel!!, I could get into serious trouble."

"Yes! Now you understand how serious this is?"

"And what was that crazy dream where I was falling and bleeding from my stomach?"

"What crazy dream? Steven, what are you talking about? What do you mean you were bleeding from your stomach?"

*

**Saturday,
6:34 a.m.**

Steven snaps out of his dream suddenly awake at home in bed. He looks to his left and sees Vicky asleep. Then he looks up at the clock on the wall... 6:34. Then he reflects on what he was dreaming of... What a long dream, he thinks. First I was jogging, then I was being chased by the police in a car chase, then I was at the batting cages thinking about it. There was something else too. What was it? Oh yeah, I was bleeding from my stomach as if I had been stabbed or shot or something. That was scary. He doesn't remember Raziel in his dream. He remembers he was talking to someone at the batting cages, and in the getaway car too. Or was I just talking to himself? Unlike other dreams he's had before this dream doesn't fade from his memory. Instead the more he tries to recall it the more vivid the details become as if they remain ready for retrieval like events that had really happened. Everything except the batting cage and whether or not he was talking to someone. That part seems fogged and the more he tries to think about it, the further it seems to slip away into oblivion.

Chapter 17

Later that same morning, in the bedroom, Steven's sits on the edge of the bed dressed in his exercise clothes, putting on his running shoes, getting ready for a morning jog. He hasn't told Vicky or the boys about his dream. As far as he's concerned, even as real as everything felt to him in this remarkable dream, it was still just a dream. With all the crazy things going on around this home right now, weird dreams is the last thing Vicky needs to hear about.

Steven and Vicky are both in a good mood this morning. Partly because of the fact that they both had a good night sleep but mostly because there wasn't even a hint of a ghost encounter through the night. At first neither of them spoke about it. Then Vicky couldn't keep it in any more. Even though she hadn't seen anything last night, she had to find out if Steven had. Steven told her he didn't see anything. And neither of them spoke about ghost haunting again hoping that maybe if they just forget about the past incidents and just ignore that they ever even happened altogether, things will return to normal. Vicky walks into the bedroom, brushing her hair and looking into the dresser mirror, she sees Steven in the reflection, tying his shoes. Then she gives a weird look.

"You need to get some new shorts," she says.

Steven stands up and looks down at his running shorts that appear to be a size or two, too small.

"What's wrong with these?" he asks.

"Nothing... 20 years ago."

"There not that old."

"Honey, it's not the wear I'm talking about. Those things went out of style years ago."

"Style? There just running shorts. I'm going out for a run. Not posing for a magazine or modeling on the runway."

"You go out in public dressed like that?"

"Ha, ha. Very funny. I'm going jogging."

Steven walks out of the room and into the kitchen. Vicky follows him.

"OK," she says, "Well you go jogging then. The boys and I are going to the store to get Teddy's sneakers and pick up a few things. Is there anything you need? Besides a wardrobe makeover?"

"Yea, make me an appointment with Renaldo, I need my eyebrows plucked and my hair done, I just can't get it to bring out my cheek bones the way he does. Oh yeah and don't forget the pedicure."

Vicky laughs at Steven's sarcasm. "Right... Well we'll be back after a while. Call me if you need anything."

"OK, be careful. Love you."

"Love you too."

They exchange a kiss and Steven heads out the front door.

"Bye, cinnamon."

"Bye, toast."

Chapter 18

It's now mid morning about 10:00 and Vicky is at Wal-Mart pushing a shopping cart through the aisles. In it are Teddy's new sneakers, and the usual household items, laundry detergent, paper towels, shampoo etc...

Erick, and Teddy have ventured out to the toys and video game departments to do their own browsing. It's not unusual for them to split up and go their own way like this when their out shopping. Vicky prefers that the boys go on their own like this so she doesn't have to hear the predictable whining, "Are we done yet?... I'm tired... Can we buy this?... When are we going home?" This way, she can take her time and focus on what she really needs to buy.

Now that Vicky is about done with her shopping she's on her way to where she suspects the boys might be. She stops by one of the stores end cap sales displaying jigsaw puzzles and begins browsing through them when her cell phone rings. She sees on her caller ID that it's Steven calling just before she answers.

"Dr. Saggin's, erectile dysfunction clinic, what's your problem?," She answers in her best Lily Tomlin operator voice.

"Uh... I think I got the wrong number." Steven says.

"Nothing to be embarrassed about sweetheart, you can always call back when you muster up the courage to deal with your problem."

"I don't have any probl..."

"That's not what your wife Victoria tells us."

"Wait a minute... Vicky?"

"Hi Steven," she says, unable to suppress her laugh.

"Wow, you got me good, Vee. Are you still at the store?"

"Yea, we're getting ready to leave soon. Did you need something?"

"I was gonna get in the shower and I noticed we're low on shampoo."

"Got it, oh and I got some more toothpaste, too. Can you think of anything else we might need?"

"No, I guess not. I just wanted to let you know about the shampoo. I'm gonna jump in the shower. See you in a while."

"OK... Oh, by the way, how was your run?"

"Exhausting. I'm so sore from yesterday. But I was expecting that to happen. Look, I gotta take a shower, I'm causing the whole house to stink like a sweat-hog locker room."

"OK, see you when we get home. Love you."

"Yeah, yeah. Just don't forget the shampoo, Toots."

Vicky smiles and Hangs up her cell phone. Then she picks out a 1000 piece difficulty jigsaw puzzle, sets it in the cart and sets off to find the boy's.

*

Back home standing in the kitchen, Steven hangs up the phone. Still grinning from the thought that Vicky was able to pull a fast one on him again, he opens the fridge and takes out a bottled water, unscrews the cap and takes a couple of swigs. Then he recaps the bottle, sets it on the counter next to the newspaper and head for the shower, when he's startled by the sound of a door slamming shut at the other side of the house. "Not this again," he thinks, and rushes to investigate.

As he suspected it was the door to the boys room. He slowly turns the knob to the door and immediately notices that there no resistance as he opens it. From the doorway he looks in the room listening silently for anything strange, prepared to parry to one side or another if something were to suddenly fly off the floor or from the top of one of the dressers but finding nothing out of the ordinary happens. He slowly walks to the closet and opens it but nothing unusual jumps out at him. Satisfied with the fact that there's nothing strange or paranormal happening here he heads for the door. When he reaches the door and goes through it the door starts to slam shut behind him, but he catches it within just a couple of inches of it slamming. Then he feels a breeze blowing through the crack of the door and he goes back into the room and closes an open window that caused the door to slam.

*

Back at the Wal-Mart, Vicky is pushing the cart and arrives to the electronics and video game section. She spots Erick looking at a video game on a shelf through a clear plastic display rack.

"Erick. Where's you brother?"

Erick walks over to Vicky.

"I think he's by the toy's, mom."

"We need to find him, it's time to go."

They push the cart a couple of aisles and spot Teddy.

"Teddy, come on . We're leaving."

Teddy holds up an action figure, showing it to his mother.

"Mom, can we buy this?"

"Put it back. Maybe for you're birthday. OK."

"Please..."

"You have a birthday coming up. You need to make a list and wait, OK."

"OK." And without any further protest, Teddy puts the action figure back on the shelf and walks to his mom.

Joey Lester is standing about 8 feet away from Teddy on his cell phone as he mimics restocking toys on shelves from a shopping basket. On the other end of the call is his buddy Jeff. Joey is talking in a normal tone and seems to be more focused on his phone call than the job stocking shelves, which he seems to be pretending to do, instead of actually doing it.

"She's just tripping bro. Give her a little time she'll come around. Trust me," Joey says.

Just then Joey turns and sees Mikey walking his way.

"Oh, crap! Gotta bounce bro."

He quickly slaps his flip phone shut and shoves it in his pocket.

Mikey has caught Joey again, trying to work and talk on his phone, and like mixing baking soda and vinegar, the two don't blend well yielding a violent reaction that just ends up making a big foamy mess. Of all the employees in the store Joey is probably the worst candidate to try and prove otherwise. Multitasking wouldn't be such a bad thing for him to attempt if only all the tasks he were focused on were aimed at the same goal. Unfortunately the tasks he chooses are pulling him in opposite directions and the direction he chooses to focus on more is the one that doesn't benefit the job he's being paid to do.

Mikey's got a small sarcastic smile on his face that somewhat disguises his disappointment, and is shaking his head as he's looking downward.

"Joey... Joey...I gotta let you know, right now. This is your last chance." he says.

Taking a defensive stance, Joey protest, "Who said I was on the phone?"

"Nobody said anything, Joey. Nobody had to. I'm not blind, you know. I can see with my own two eyes."

"Mikey, I swear. I was only on the phone for a couple of seconds. It ain't hurting anybody."

"Look, that's not the point," Mikey says, with no intention of debating what he saw.

"But..."

"Joey," Mikey cuts him off, "I'm gonna give you some advice and I don't want you to take this personally. But if you can't stay off the phone, then maybe you need a different kind of job. One that lets you talk on the phone all day if you want."

"Mikey, I'm not on the phone all day..."

"Look, just do us both a big favor and shut your phone off while you're here at work."

"But what if there's an emergency?" Joey asks.

"If there's an emergency your family can reach you by calling the store. I'm pretty sure they'll have no problem getting a hold of you that way. The point is, if I keep letting you get away with it, eventually another manager is gonna report me. Then I'll get reprimanded, put on report. And I don't need a bad mark on my record just because you can't follow the rules."

"I know, but it was only..."

"Joey! Stop! Please. Just stay off the phone while you're on the clock. OK? I don't care what you do after you clock, but as long as you're on company time please stay off the phone."

"OK, but..."

"Thank you."

Mikey walks away.

*

In another part of the store, Vicky is pushing the cart through the main aisle, and the boys are following along side of her. Teddy looks in the cart basket and sees the puzzle and pulls it out.

"Wait a minute...Who is this for?" he asks.

"It was on sale, Vicky says, "It's for all of us... I think it'll be something fun for all of us to do."

"Cool. Let me see," Erick says, reaching for the puzzle.

They pass through the clothing department and Vicky spots men's gym shorts, which reminds her of the ugly shorts Steven was wearing this morning. She picks up a pair of light blue shorts and holds them out so she can get a better look.

"Now this is more the style of the times," she says.

"Are those for Dad?" Erick asks.

"They sure are. He needs them," Vicky says, "What do you think?"

"He'll never wear those," Teddy says.

"Sure he will," Vicky says, "Why do you say he won't?"

Erick finds a pair of dark blue shorts and holds them up, showing them to his mom.

"Get him these," he says.

"And throw away the old ones," Teddy adds.

Not surprised that she wasn't the only one who noticed how ridiculous Steven looked in the old shorts he was wearing earlier, Vicky cracks a small smile as she asks, "You saw them, huh?"

Teddy nods his head.

"That's a good idea," she says.

Chapter 19

The white mini SUV pulls into the driveway and parks next to Steven's work car. Vicky and the boys get out, open the hatchback and start unloading shopping bags.

In the house Steven is sitting in the living room with the TV on and looking at the newspaper as the front door opens and Teddy walks wearing his new shoes and carrying in one hand a bag with what looks like a shoe box in it, and a fast food soda cup in the other. Erick who's carrying a bag of miscellaneous house products and a soda, comes in after him then Vicky carrying a couple more bags.

They all set the bags on the dining room table. And as Vicky begins emptying the bags and putting things away. She sees the bag with Teddy's old shoes on the table.

"Teddy don't leave your old shoes here," she tells him.

"What should I do with them?"

"Take them out to the trash. You're not gonna wear them anymore. I don't even know why we brought them home."

Teddy starts to leave with the bag and Vicky notices the kitchen trash can is full so she stops him.

"Teddy, wait," she says.

Vicky pulls the plastic kitchen trash liner full of trash from the kitchen trash can and hands it to Teddy. "Since your going out to the trash can, you might as well take this with you."

Vicky goes into the living room and sit on the couch next to Steven.

"Hey, Burger... see any ghost today?"

"Thank God, no ghost to speak of today, Coke."

"Coke?"

"Burger and Coke are good together."

"I would've thought you were gonna say Fries."

"Yeah, Fries are good too, but I like my Burger with a Coke."

"Well, anyway, no ghost is good news, right? Whatcha reading about?"

"Ah, nothing," Steven answers, "Just looking at the movie times."

"Movies!?"

"Yeah, that movie the kids want to see came out a couple of weeks ago. I was thinking maybe we should go tonight. Before we're totally broke."

"Sounds like fun... I'm pretty sure the boy's will like that."

Chapter 20

Friday,
10:00 p.m.

Joey, Jeff and Carl are hanging out at the corner of 7th Street and Adams. Carl works this street, routinely selling cocaine to the rich folks or anyone else looking to buy.

He's convinced he has a foolproof system, guaranteed to make them a good handful of money to get those extra toys, like boom box speakers for the car, a gold chain now and then, the latest iphone device, and money left over to party on the weekend. The plan is as follows: Make a drug sale or two, then move to a different corner a block or two away. Make two more sales then move again. Work three different locations, two rounds and call it a night. Split the profit three ways, sell again another day. Never two days in a row. Don't give any discounts. Don't try and make any big deals. Don't get greedy. He needs two lookouts (Jeff and Joey). One person with a gun to make them look gangsta, just to hold their own in case things get a little rough. Carl controls the negotiations. Jeff and Joey take turns holding the gun, switching each time they change locations.

Right now it's Joeys turn to hold the gun, and he stands guard where he can clearly be seen as a silhouette in the shadows at the corner near by.

*

At a movie theater about a mile from where Joey and his buddies are dealing; Steven, Vicky and the boys are walking to their car having finished watching a movie.

"So what did you think guys? Was that a good movie or what?" Steven asks.

"That movie was awesome!" Teddy says excitedly.

"It was sick, dad!" Erick chimes in.

"Sick? So what are you saying? You didn't like it?" Steven asks.

"Dad... Sick means it was good," Teddy says.

Steven smiles at the boys. Sometimes he likes to pretend he doesn't understand the latest lingo just to stir the pot, and keep the dialog going. Then he gets a laugh from listening to them put him in his place.

"I'm just kidding with you guys... I know what it means."

They walk a couple of more steps, then Steven gets an idea to keep the night going well. "I say we should stop at the store and buy some chopped nuts, fudge and whip cream, go home and dig into that tub of ice cream mom bought today. What do you think guys?"

Erick cheers, "Cool! Ice cream!"

Teddy adds, "This is a perfect day!"

They reach the white Ford Escape and Steven gets in the driver side, Vicky in the front passenger side and the boys in back.

*

Back near 7th and Adams, two undercover police men are staked out in a parked unmarked car in a dark space watching traffic but more important to them is the group of three young men they've been watching and suspect are selling narcotics at a corner.

Although the three suspects are the current objective and the reason they are here at this particular time and place, the conversation they're currently engaged in, is about a situation that occurred a few months ago. Officer Baines in the driver seat seems to be doing the most talking, "...So I had the guy in a lock hold but he still had the gun in his hand, then the idiot shot me in the leg, so I broke his arm to make him drop the gun. And get this, are you ready for this. You're not gonna believe this. He got a lawyer and now I'm getting sued for brutality. Can you believe this crap?"

Officer Garner, who is sitting in the front passenger seat of the unmarked cop car, says, "Lawyers are just as bad if not worse then the scum their defending.

"Unless it's their house or business that's being robbed," Baines adds.

They see a silver BMW drive by and slow down at the corner they're watching.

"OK, partner... That's our guy... Get ready," Garner says.

The silver BMW pulls up to the curb next to

where the Joey, Jeff and Carl are standing spaced about 10 to 15 feet apart. A hidden radio in the BMW transmits the exchange of dialog taking place at the corner, to Garner and Baines as well as another group of cops with handheld radios in a van recording it all not far from the scene.

Driving the BMW is Officer Kent, working undercover, dressed in street clothes, you wouldn't be able to recognize him as a cop yet alone the one in charge of this operation. He's been watching this gang work this corner for over a week now. He knows they're small time dealers. He's already seen enough and knows taking them down will pose no serious danger. Once he has the group contained he plans to separate the individuals of the small gang and convince them that it would be in their best interest to snitch out their supplier.

He leans towards the open passenger window to talk to the gang leader. "Hey Holmes, any of you know where I can score a hit?" he asks, acting like he's already slightly intoxicated.

"Sorry cop. Can't help you," Carl says. He always plays this card with buyers he's never met, and he's never been arrested, so it must be working. His theory is if it's a cop, letting him know that his cover is blown, will likely send him on his way, which is also raises the red flag for the gang to stash the goods and close shop for the night.

Kent doesn't take the bluff, he stays in character and says, "Look man, I'm not asking you to sell me anything. I'm just asking around to see if anyone knows where I can score a good time for myself and some friends. Were having some ladies over a little later and I'm just looking for a little something that will help relax everyone, get them in the mood, you know..."

Carl still not completely convinced remains a little suspicious and is looking around to see if they're being watched. He asks, "How much, you got, dude?"

"I got $200," Kent say's as he thumbs through a couple of fifties and twenties.

Though he's never seen this guy before, his flow of regulars don't seem to be out in their usual numbers right now and it looks like this could be a slow night. Maybe a new customer or two could be good for business. Pulling his closed fist out of his pocket Carl reaches it into the open window of the BMW. Kent holds up the $200 and Carl takes it between his thumb and forefinger and drops the small balloon wrapped ball in Kent's other hand.

"Thanks man you're a life saver. What do you call yourself?" Kent says. Which is also happens to be the preplanned signal word for all units to move in and make the arrest.

Chapter 21

Parked across the street, the two cops recognize the signal word.

"That's the signal, let's move!" says Garner.

Wearing bulletproof flack vest with the word "POLICE" in white letters on their backs, the cops both jump out of the car and run across the street to make the arrest. Two other cops also dressed the same appear rushing in from around the opposite corner.

Jeff spots the cops running towards him and shouts to warn Carl and Joey. "Police! Beat it!"

As soon as Joey hears the word police, he takes off running down Adams street as fast as his legs will carry him.

Jeff tries to make a break to his left on 7th street, but is immediately tackled down by two other undercover cops he didn't see.

Carl struggles to escape but is handcuffed and

easily held in place by Officer Kent through the window of the car, as one of the two cops from the car across the street arrives and manages to get a hold of him from behind and get him settled down.

Garner, went running down Adams street, in pursuit of Joey who's already had a good head start, but isn't in shape to run very far at the pace he's on. Joey started down Adams street and cut left in an alley between 8th and 9th street. He gets about 30 yards and ducks behind a dumpster breathing hard.

*

Traffic moves by slowing down at the corner where a couple of squad cars are stopped with their red and blue lights flashing, drawing the interest of a few onlookers as well as the people riding by and looking out their windows to see what's happening. Among them Steven, Vicky and the boys in their white SUV.

"Looks like something's happening up there," Steven says.

"An accident?" Vicky asks.

"I don't think so," says Steven as he notices the two young men sitting on the curb with their hands cuffed. The two men sitting on the curb kind of remind him of the dream he had last night, but he doesn't notice the silver BMW parked right in front of them as he needs to turn his attention to the traffic he's driving through. "Looks like a drug bust, maybe. Look, guys, check it out."

Remembering more about the dream Steven remembers that he was in a police chase not long after he saw the two men apprehended on the sidewalk curb. Then thinking about it more he realizes that the young men look like the exact same guys he dreamed of just last night. Now he sees the parked BMW and he tries to look to see if anyone is in the front seat of the BMW but the traffic flow picks up and cars start blowing their horns so he has to drive on which prevents him from getting a close enough look.

Erick and Teddy are sitting in the back seat. They both look out the window to see what's happening. As they drive away from the silver BMW, Erick looks back notices there is a man in the driver seat. The man looks strangely like his dad but Erick doesn't say anything about it.

Everything about this reminds Steven about the dream he had. It's a busy part of town... the silver BMW... the two thugs handcuffed on the curb... and all the cops, everything is just as he remembered it was in his dream. Trying to get his mind off of the crazy idea that he would somehow be able to see the future in his dream, Steven tells the boys, "You see that boys? That's what happens when you don't finish school... You start hanging out with the wrong crowd and sooner or later the police will catch you doing something wrong."

*

Waiting in the alley hidden behind the dumpster, for the cop who went after him to show himself, Joey has caught his breath and is now resting quietly. He takes the gun out of his pocket, holds it in his right hand and checks to make sure the safety is off. Then he aims it toward Adams street.

The cop runs up to where Adams street intersects with the alley in both directions and stops.

He waits for a moment looking and listening for any movement from all three directions. He knows this is the intersection where his assailant must have changed directions. But just as evident is the fact that he couldn't have gotten beyond this area without leaving a clue as to which way he went next. Not unless he's hiding somewhere close by.

Joey holds his position shaking nervously holding his breath and pointing the gun directly at the cop. The cop pulls out his gun and starts down the alley getting closer to Joey. With the gun in his right hand Joey remains hidden. He uses his other hand to steady his aim looking down the sight directly at the cops head. "He's just another troublemaker punking my game," he thinks to himself, "This piece of crap deserves a bullet in the head." There's no hammer to cock back on the automatic handgun so the only sound the cop will hear will be the sound of the gun firing just before the bullet exit's the other side of his head. Joey feels his pressure of his finger preparing to squeeze the trigger.

Chapter 22

Carl and Jeff sit on the curb, hands cuffed behind their backs. Two other undercover cops are standing by them talking to each other and Officer Kent is talking with Officer Baines and a uniformed patrol officer at the front of a patrol car with lights flashing that happens to be parked directly behind the silver BMW. On the hood of the patrol car are the confiscated drugs taken from Carl's pocket and found in a bag hidden behind a newspaper stand on the same corner.

During their conversation about the drug arrest, Baines happens to glance into the BMW and he sees someone in the driver seat. "Hey, what the...!!!" he shouts.

Then the car starts the car up and screeches away. "The car!!" Kent hollers. And Baines yells into his hand held radio.

*

"Garner! Garner! You need you to get back here ASAP!" Garners radio blares out, causing Joey to hesitate and not fire the gun he's aiming at Garners head. Garner knows the loud radio transmission has just blown his chances of finding and catching the third suspect, but it doesn't matter anymore. Evidently something bigger is happening back at the original crime scene and he needs to get back 7th and Adams where he's needed. "Garner, 10-4. I'm breaking pursuit and coming back your way," He radios back as he turns around and goes running back up Adams street.

Joey breaths a sigh of relief, hands shaking, he sets the guns safety back on, tucks the it in the back of his pants and pulls his shirt over it. He stands up takes off the hoodie he was wearing to change his appearance in hope that the absence of the hoodie will make enough of a difference so that he won't match the description of the perpetrator the police are after. Then he tosses it in the trash and jogs away, in the opposite direction.

*

Steven, Vicky and the boys continue driving and when they're about 6 blocks away, they hear the police siren wailing from behind them. Steven slows down and stops at a red light, and looks into the rear view mirror to see what's happening behind them.

Just then the silver BMW pulls up right next to them. But because Steven is looking into the rearview mirror, he doesn't see it. Teddy recognizes that it's the same car that the police had pulled over a few blocks back. He sees the driver of the BMW quickly looking left and right into the intersection. The driver looks at the SUV briefly then into his rearview mirror then back at the SUV where he sees Teddy in the back seat looking right at him. Teddy sees the driver and immediately recognizes that it's his dad driving the BMW. If it were only that this man looked like his dad, Teddy would have been able to dismiss him as an identical stranger, something that's bound to happen once in your life. But there was something more. This man in the other car, was wearing the same shirt his dad was, his mannerism were so similar to what he would expect from his own dad had he been in the same predicament. But more than anything else was the fact that the driver in the other car immediately recognize Teddy looking back at him. Stunned with confusion from seeing the dissonant involvement of his dad with crime, Teddy momentarily forgets that his dad is sitting right in front of him in the same car. "Dad?" he says, nervously.

Steven responds by turning to his right and looking back at where Teddy is seated. "What's up, Teddy? Are you OK?," He asks.

The driver of the silver BMW peels out and through the red light cutting in front of Steven's car making a right turn then quickly speeding away. Steven is looks at the car screeching away but still doesn't see the driver. Then he looks over at Vicky who's bracing herself. She didn't see the driver either but is now watching the car drive away.

"Are you guys OK back there?" He asks the boys.

"I hope they catch that crazy maniac before he kills someone," Vicky says.

"Maniac," she called him, Teddy thinks to himself, she didn't see his face. Brought back to reality, Teddy knows his dad is sitting right in front of him. But that other man looked just like him. Dad would never be involved with those thugs. If it were him being chased by the police, he wouldn't make them chase him like that. He would just pull over and talk with them. But it was him. It looked just like him. And it seemed like he knew who I was too.

The police siren fades away as Steven, Vicky and the boys get their green light and continue their drive home.

Chapter 23

Tammy, Bryan and Stanley are the road crew for the local Channel 3 weekend news. Currently they are riding in the Channel 3 new van on the freeway driving back to the station from doing a follow up story for the 10:00 news about a hero dog that saved his owners life by alerting a neighbors to come to her aid after she had passed out in the kitchen from heat stress.

It's been a pretty slow month for weekend news stories and this Saturday didn't started much different from the last. When they received the phone call from the neighbor about the hero dog, they took on the gig mostly because they had nothing better to go on, but partly just to get out of the studio and out on the road where sometimes just being in the right place at the right time you might get lucky and catch a lightning strike on camera. As for the hero dog story, it went off without a hitch. First the interview with the recovering pet owner in the hospital bed, then the good Samaritan neighbor with the dog out in front of the hospital due to the fact that pets were not allowed inside.

Reporter Tammy Marshal has been growing tired what she feels has been a dead end career so far. She doesn't want to grow old working in this station for the rest of her life. Her dream is to land an anchor position and get recognized by the parent network out in Los Angeles. Then one day be selected for a job out in New York in a national broadcasting station. But without the big story she'll never even gain notoriety from this small station.

After shooting a story and returning the company van, the crew typically goes out for the evening for drinks at a bar in Angelo's Restaurant to celebrate and discuss how things went or how things could have gone better. Right now Tammy's riding quietly reflecting about her career and wondering when her big story will strike.

"Going to Angelo's tonight?" Bryan asks, from the back seat.

"Probably not." Tammy says, from the front passenger seat.

"What? Why not?"

"I don't know, just not in the mood I guess."

"Awe, come on, you might as well just say you're too good to hang out with us low life's, or something like that."

"I'm too good to hang out with you low life's."

"Dude... I can't believe you just said that. What about you Stanley?"

Driving the van and looking in the rear view mirror, Stanley answers, "I don't know, maybe... Hey guys, it looks like there's something big coming our way."

Tammy and Bryan both turn around, look out the back window and see the flashing red and blue lights of police cars about a quarter mile back approaching rather fast. Then they see the silver BMW out in front in the lead, lit up by a helicopter spotlight and also approaching at top speed weaving though traffic and cutting lanes just barely missing the other cars, and passing them as if they were standing still. As the BMW gets closer they can see that the man driving the car seems to be talking aloud to someone.

"Looks like he's on a speaker phone with someone," Tammy says.

"Could be talking with his crime buddies or something," Bryan says.

"Or the media," Stanley says.

As the car speeds by them on their left the helicopter spot light from above brightens up the entire road and they can hear the sound of the helicopter from overhead. They get a clear view of the driver and notice he seems to be looking at their van and the other cars in their flow of traffic. Bryan has the camera on and is filming the car as it passes by. The BMW continues ahead taking with it the brightness of the spotlight and the sound of helicopter, then they hear the sound of the police sirens approaching from the rear and in no time the squad cars are right there next to them. About ten car lengths ahead of them the silver getaway car suddenly cuts across to the right causing all traffic in the two right lanes to come to a screeching halt as he just makes it into the exit ramp to Theodore Avenue. The patrol car following him was picking up speed on him so fast that he wasn't able to slow down in time to make the turn off and catch the off ramp. Instead he ended up slamming on his brakes bringing the patrol car to a complete stop and tried backing up against traffic which made traffic slow down even more. They watched the BMW cut a hard right turn on the off ramp and almost lose control as it reaches the left turn in the middle of the "S" turn then speed up. More patrol cars speed past them on the right shoulder and in the freeway off ramp.

"Stanley get us over there, now! GO! GO! GO!" Tammy shouts.

As traffic slowly resumes, Tammy opens her window and leans out holding her hand out signaling and shouting to the other cars to halt and let them by. Stanley maneuvers the Channel 3 van to the shoulder of the freeway and speeds to the off ramp.

"Hurry! We're gonna lose them!"

"I'm not losing my license for interfering with a police car chase!" Stanley shouts.

He slows the van to a stop at end of the "S" turn off ramp exit, before making the right turn onto Theodore Avenue.

"Come on Stanley, don't stop' there's no other traffic here, grow a pair and put the pedal to the metal!" Bryan says.

"Relax we're not going to lose them. I'll lay two to one odds that they already have more patrol cars to heading him off from Allesandro."

"Allesandro?"

"Yeah, this road dead ends at the base of the mountain at Allesandro and heads back into Moreno Valley. The only other way out is if he reaches the Allesandro East outlet before the cops do."

"What are you talking about?"

"I know these roads, and I'm betting the cops have him trapped already."

"Bryan get the camera ready." Tammy says.

"I'm way ahead of you," Bryan says as he's loading a fresh battery in the camera and one in his pocket.

Stanley steps harder on the accelerator pedal and as they speed toward the flashing lights and they see the police cars have both lanes blocked and the BMW is stopped side ways in the middle of the road. On the other side of the silver car are more patrol cars facing it with their headlights and spot lights on and all aimed at the getaway car. The helicopter is still circling overhead with the spotlight beaming down brightening up what would normally be a dark secluded road. The man seems to be sitting still in the driver seat with both hands on the wheel. It's hard for anyone to see what the driver looks like because of the glare from the backwash of lights coming from the opposite sides of the BMW. Stopping short of where all the police cars are, Stanley puts the van into park and Tammy gets out of the van with Bryan following closely with camera on his shoulder filming as they make their way to the nearest patrol car for cover. They can see the silhouette of the man still in the driver seat of the silver car.

They watch and film from a safe spot behind one of the patrol cars as the police stand position from both sides of the silver car with their pistols aimed at the driver seat. Watching they wait for the perpetrator to be removed from the car and taken down so they can come out from behind the patrol car for their big story. And as they hear one of the officers probably the one in charge call out for the driver to show his hands, then they see him duck down in the car.

"Are you getting this?," Tammy asks Bryan.

"I couldn't get a clear focus on the guy in the

car."

"Are you kidding me? With all these lights?"

"That's the problem, there's too much light. Mainly coming from the other side. It's causing him to appear as a shadow in the camera's eye!"

"Oh my god."

With the spotlight and headlights from the patrol cars on the opposite side the camera isn't able to get a clear picture of the perpetrator nor were they able to accurately see what he looked like. Now that he's ducked down and out of view they'll have to wait till the police are able to get him out of the car.

The police call out again for the driver to show his hands, but get no response. So they make their move, closing in on the front seat of the car. The cop on the passenger side of the car motions for the one on the driver side to move in closer, which he does and when he gets to the window he reaches in turns the car off and retrieves the keys and takes them to the trunk.

"Something's not right," Tammy says.

"What makes you think that?" Bryan asks as he films.

"They didn't take the guy out of the car, and now they're opening the trunk. Did the guy commit suicide or something? What happened to him?"

They see the cops looking around and under the car as if they lost something, but nobody in hand cuffs as they all lower and holster their weapons.

"Let's go," Tammy says. And they all get up and head for the BMW, only to be headed off by a cop who stops them from getting any closer. "Sorry, I can't let you get any closer guys, this is still an active crime scene."

"Officer, did you guys make an arrest? Where's

the perpetrator? Is he alive?" Tammy asks holding out a microphone.

"Sorry, I'm not the man you want to interview," He says as he opens the trunk to one of the patrol cars and pulls out a yellow roll of police crime scene tape.

*

Over an hour has past and Tammy and her crew have been waiting for an interview with anyone who can give them some answers. It appears as if something or someone has possibly outsmarted the authorities and has them totally baffled. Or they're trying to cover up an arrest gone wrong. Nobody has been apprehended, no sign of violence, no drugs, no stolen money or jewels and yet the silver BMW is taped off as a crime scene and being dusted for fingerprints. Tammy called her boss back at the station and he authorized the overtime and told her to stay at the crime scene till they get the story.

Officer Kent finally walks over towards Tammy. She sees him coming and composes herself for the interview. But Kent waves his hands signaling her not to film.

"Don't film this, I want to talk to you off camera first," he says, "Off the record."

"Am I going to get a story on the record?" Tammy asks.

"If you want the truth, let me give it to you then you can decide if you even have a story you want to run with."

Kent tells Tammy and her crew the whole story from the drug bust to the stolen car to the end of the car chase, and finishes with, "Nobody knows how he got away or where he went to, but even though he somehow managed to slip from our capture this time, we'll catch up to him because they have plenty of fingerprints lifted from the vehicle inside and out.

"Can we take a look at the video footage you have?"

"We'll show it to you. You can even have a copy. But the original is ours protected by freedom of the press."

"Yeah, yeah... Spare me the politics, I just want to see if you caught him on film. None of my men got a view of what this guy looked like."

"We saw him!," Bryan says.

"What color was his hair?" Kent asks.

"Brown!" "Red!" "Blonde!" The three news crew witnesses say at the same time.

"Was his hair long or short?"

"Long!" Short!" "Curly!... I think."

"So was he Caucasian?"

"Yes!" "No!" "I... couldn't tell."

"Alright. I can see you guys are quite observant. You haven't been drinking tonight by any chance, have you?"

"Look you asked us what we saw... and..."

"Relax, don't worry about it. None of my men can say what this guy looked like either. And they all had guns drawn and aimed right at him. Can we take a look at the video you have?"

Bryan plugs a wire to the camera and into a control panel in the van that has a small color monitor. Then he rewinds the video back to the part where the police had the car stopped. Looking at the video the silver car comes in and out of focus but the figure inside behind the wheel is never clear enough to make out what he looks like.

"What's wrong with your camera?," Kent asks.

"It's not the camera. There was too much light coming in from behind the car and the camera's auto focus was going haywire trying to get the picture."

"Did you get anything else?"

"Yeah, on the freeway... Let me rewind it some more."

Bryan rewinds it back to where the chase passed them on the freeway then hit the play button. The monitor shows the silver car approaching fast but the front windshield is giving off a glare from the helicopter spotlight from above that flares out right in front of the drivers face. As the car passes from the side, it appears as if they're going to get a good view of what the driver looks like but then more glare from the side windows prevent the camera from seeing the inside of the car and instead they just see a reflection of part of the channel 3 news van in the window.

"I don't know how that could be?... When I filmed it I had a clear shot of the driver right when he passed us," Bryan says.

Kent can't believe what's happening. All these people and not one reliable witness. Professionals, all of them. Everybody saw it happen with their own two eyes and nobody seems to have gotten a real picture of what this guy looks like.

"Well, at least we have fingerprints."

Just then one of the officers walks up to Kent and the TV crew as they're talking and Kent sees him.

"Sergeant Kent?" the other cop calls as he's walking towards him.

"Ah, here we go," Kent says " What do we have?"

"We took all the prints we retrieved from the vehicle and ran them through the system."

"Now we're talking... What do we know?"

"Well sir, the test can't be ruled as conclusive just yet... we'll get better results when we get back in the lab."

"Come on, tell me... What do we got?"

"Sir it would probably be better if..."

"Just tell me. What do we know?!"

"Sir, all the fingerprints we lifted belong to you."

"What?"

"I know. It's the craziest thing. Even the prints on the steering wheel are yours. Most of them aren't even smudged. Even if the other person were wearing gloves, they would have either wiped off or smudged your prints. But that didn't happen. It's as if nobody but you were ever in that car. "

Chapter 24

At home later that night Steven is home in bed getting ready to fall asleep and he remembers the drive home from the movies. The silver BMW seemed very much like the one that was in his dream. Then he remembers how he drove it through the busy street in town and saw himself and Vick and the boys in their car at the stoplight. Then he remembered Teddy seeing him. As he thinks about his past dream he tiredly falls asleep and begins dreaming.

Standing alone atop a mountain overlooking the city at night, Steven looks down and admires the city lights. Then he looks up into the night sky and notices Raziel is standing next to him.

"Steven we need to talk about your dreams," She says with an unusual urgency.

"Yes, Raziel, I have a few questions of my own."

"Steven, your dream traveling."

"Yeah, you said that to me before... What does that mean?"

"It means your dreams are taking you to places

and times that are real."

"Real? So what? Doesn't everyone dream of real places?"

"This is different, Steven. Your not just dreaming of the places. You're actually at places that are real, interacting with real people doing things that are real. You've been to the real future."

"Future?"

"Steven. No one but God knows the future. And once you've seen it, it's no longer a future, but a part of your past. It will inevitably happen. You might not like what you see, but there will be nothing you can do to stop it from happening. I can't tell you what your future is because I don't even know it. The future is yours to choose. But once you see it, becomes a part of your past. Like a prophecy. And once it becomes that, there's no changing it. Every path you take, every decision you make, every obstacle you encounter will inevitably lead you to that event, just as you saw it happen."

Steven knows that he's in a dream right now. But he also knows that the dream he had the other night of himself jogging, had a different feel to it. And the events that unfolded around him stayed true to the rules of life unlike the imaginary batting cage in which he was able to control whether it looked old and tattered or brand new, or like here on the mountain top where he's able to conjure shooting stars at will.

"Is that's why they feel so real."

Steven looks around and even though he's pretty sure this place isn't real he asks, "So this place. Is it real?"

"No. This place is imaginary."

They both begin walking as Steven looks around.

"You said, I've been to the future, right?"

"Yes."

So what year am I in now?"

"Like I said. This place isn't real, so the time here isn't real."

Suddenly Steven notices, that although it is still night, he and Raziel are no longer atop the mountain, but now are now walking on a pier by the ocean. There's a man sitting on a foldout chair babysitting 2 fishing poles leaning on the rails with lines extending down into the water.

"Did I do this?" Steven asks.

"Yes. You brought us here."

"But I didn't choose to be here. It just happened."

"That's the way dreams work Steven. I never said you had power to choose when or where your dreams take you."

Steven looks around as he and Raziel walk towards the end of the pier, and senses the difference now. He smells the fresh saltwater in the air feels the cool moisture breeze as it blows a mist on his face. Goose bumps form on his arms from the surging drop in temperature.

"Is this place real?" He asks.

"Yes! Just like when you were being chased by the police the other night."

"Wait... That's right. That's when you first told me I was dream traveling. When I was driving the car. That was real?!"

The fisherman sees only Steven walking by, talking out loud to himself. He's not phased by it much. It's about 3 o'clock in the morning and he's seen this kind of thing before. He shakes his head, thinking Steven is probably some kind of schizophrenic.

"So can I go to the past too. Can I see the history of the world?," Steven asks.

"You haven't dream traveled to the past yet. But usually the way it works is, you can only dream travel to places where you have been or will be."

Steven stops at the rail of the pier and looks down to the water.

"How am I supposed to know if the place I'm dreaming of, is real or not?"

"Most of the places you've dreamed of have been imaginary. But recently your dreams have been taking you to places that are real. Steven, you can sense the realness right now. I know you do. And I know you felt it when the police were chasing you. That's partly why you were so anxious to escape."

Before their conversation can go any further Steven dream travels from the pier and both he and Raziel are no longer there.

The fisherman didn't see Steven disappear but he notices now that he isn't around anymore and he gets up and hurries to the corner of the pier where he last saw him. Looking left and right then over the pier rail and down into the water, he shakes his head in disgust and grunts, "He's probably better off now."

*

Steven dream travels back 26 years into his past. He's 9 years old again and the reality is that he's at his Grandma Lee's house watching Saturday morning cartoons. He notices the smell of bacon and toast in the air but it doesn't phase him from watching cartoons. Raziel isn't with him now and he's so comfortable with being here that he forgets he's a dream traveler in this part of the real world. He doesn't realize it but Grandma Lee is in the kitchen just finishing up her late morning cleaning routine. Not a care in the world he sits comfortably focused on the cartoons playing on the tube.

Then he hears Grandma Lee call to him, "Steven... Stevie."

Steven stands up and looks at her. "Wait a minute," he thinks to himself, How can this be possible?" The fact that his grandma is alive and is right here in person is totally remarkable to say the least. This couldn't be real. Not if she's here in person. She passed away years ago. He feels goose bumps start to form on his arms. But this all seems so real. Looking around at the walls and the furniture he sees that everything is really there. In a dream he wouldn't be able to create this house exactly the way it is now. There's no way he could dream this house with the detail he see's it now. This is real. He's slightly confused and disoriented but he doesn't say anything. He just curiously looks at her wondering to himself how this could be possible.

"Do you want something to snack on, maybe a peanut butter and jelly sandwich or something."

"Sure Grandma," He replies not because he's hungry but mostly because he doesn't want to seem disrespectful by rejecting her.

"OK." she says, and goes to the cupboard and retrieves the peanut butter.

Something still seems odd to Steven. He's not quite sure what it is. But something is definitely out of whack here.

"Grandma Lee in the kitchen?" he thinks to himself... "Grandma Lee... this is impossible. She died 10 years ago...this can't be real."

Again he smells the lingering odor of bacon and toast from breakfast having been cooked recently. He feels the warmth from the room comforting his arms which were covered in goose bumps just a moment ago.

Starting to feel terrified, he walks over to his grandmother, who is now fixing his sandwich.

When he reaches the kitchen, and finds himself standing right next to her, he nervously extends his hand and touches her. He feels the movement of her arm the warmth of her skin.

"Grandma?" he asks, with a little nervous tension in his voice.

Grandma Lee doesn't notice Steven's unusual behavior as she continues fixing his sandwich and answers him calmly, "Yes?"

The feel of her skin in his hand confirms it. "She's real!," He thinks to himself.

Steven is overwhelmed in emotion over the idea that his grandmother who died 10 years ago is alive! He believed he would never see her in this world again. And yet here she is standing right next to him! He can't believe this is happening. But it is. He hugs her as he takes a deep breath begins crying, "You're real... Grandma, you're alive, you're alive... you're here, you're really here! And you're alive!"

He continues hugging and weeping uncontrollably as Grandma consoles him with a hug of her own as she asks him, "What's the matter with you?... What's wrong?"

Then everything fades away as Steven wakes up from his dream.

*

At home in bed asleep Steven is still whimpering uncontrollably. Vicky hears him and realizes he's dreaming and tries to wake him up.

"Steven, sweetheart. Baby... wake up, you're dreaming."

Steven snaps out of his dream and his emotional feelings.

"Are you OK?" Vicky asks.

Steven wipes the tears from his eyes and composes himself.

"Oh my God... What a dream," He says. He's slightly embarrassed to be seen this emotional over a dream, and nervously he laughs. "I had dream I was younger and my grandma was alive. It seemed so real. At first I thought... this must be a dream, than I touched her. I actually touched her. With my hand. And I could feel her. And I hugged her. She was real, Vicky! And just kept telling her she was alive over and over, because I couldn't believe it. I'm telling you she felt so real."

"Are you OK?"

"Of coarse. I'm fine. I know it was just a dream... But it all felt so real. I could even smell the toast and bacon."

"Toast and bacon? If you ask me I'd say it sounds like somebody woke up hungry."

Chapter 25

Sunday morning.

Steven and Vicky are members of the same church their parents went to and are regulars in attendance at least 2 to 3 times a month. They have made attending church a ritualistic part of their lives since before they got married and as long as the can remember, and they both decided they want to pass the tradition down to their children. Stevens model has always been to lead the way by example. So he takes his family to church with the belief that one day when Erick and Teddy grow up, they will keep the tradition going and take their kids.

Everyone in the house is getting dressed up. Vicky usually prepares the boys clothes the night before and sets their outfits aside on a couple of the dining room chairs making it so they can't complain they don't have anything to wear.

Steven in the bathroom facing his reflection the mirror combing his hair, as Teddy walks in.

"What's up Teddy?"

"Mom say's to ask you, if you can you fix my hair?"

"Sure, come here."

Teddy stands in front of his dad facing the

mirror. There's nothing unusual about this routine which has been performed so many times before, that both Steven and Teddy would probably be able to wear blindfolds right now and still get it right.

"Teddy, you're getting tall," Steven says. Then he jokes, "Pretty soon I'm gonna be combing your hair like this." Steven raises his hands up with the comb and pretends to be combing a 7 foot tall Teddy. Then acting like he's finished, he says, "There, you're done. You can stand up now."

Teddy lets out a small laugh, as Steven goes back to combing his hair. Then Vicky comes in the bathroom holding up the back of her own hair.

"Sweetheart could you zip up the back of my dress please?" she asks.

Steven finishes combing Teddy's hair.

"We're done. Come here, turnaround, I'll zip you up."

He zips up the back of Vicky's dress.

"Are we running late?" He asks her.

"Yes," she answers.

"Why can't we ever make it to church on time?"

*

It's a warm clear and sunny. Sunday morning church service has just dismissed and Church members and visitors are standing around conversing in small groups, some are walking to their cars. Some of the kids are running around playing on the front lawn. Steven and his friend Alex are standing and talking just outside the main entrance.

"Hey, did you hear about that police chase last night," Alex asks.

"Funny, you should mention it," Steven says, "I

think the guy they were chasing passed right by us as we were coming home from the movies. Scared the life out of Vicky and me. How did you hear about it?"

"I saw it on the news this morning... So you say they passed right by you. Where were you when that happened?"

"We were on 7th street, just a few blocks from the movie theater. Did they say if they caught the guy?"

"That's the crazy part of it all. The guy didn't even give the police a very long chase. He was on the freeway for about 5 miles and the TV new channel were on the same freeway and filmed the car passing right by them.

"They did? So did they show what he looked like on camera?"

"That's what was so incredible about it."

"What do you mean?"

"You won't believe this, but they had the camera filming the car from about three feet away, and the window of the car reflected glare from the lights blocking what the driver looked like from being filmed."

"What about the car?"

"That's funny too. The car was stolen. But it belonged to one of the cops from an undercover drug sting."

"So what happened? Did they catch him?"

"He got off the freeway on Theodore Avenue, drove about half a mile and stopped the car in the middle of the road, then... get this...they say he disappeared."

"Disappeared? You mean he escaped?"

"No, he didn't escape. He disappeared."

"Disappeared?... You already said that. What do

you mean disappeared?... Wait... did you say Theodore Avenue?"

"Yes, out in the middle of nowhere. The police had the car surrounded before he had time to get out run. He disappeared inside the car. Like Houdini or something They even had news footage of him in the car before he disappeared."

"Really? Could they see what he looked like?

"No, All you could see was his shadow. The police even had the car surrounded with spotlights all around it and nobody could clearly say what he looked likel."

Steven feels a chill up his spine hearing the remarkable similarities to the dream he had the night before the police chase actually happened.

"Did the police say what he looked like?"

"No, the news people said police wouldn't comment on what the guy looked like, all they said was that he stole the car that was being used during a drug sting operation and the investigation is still pending. But if you ask me, I'd say that whoever this car thief is, he's the best at what he does because he was surrounded by the police and they even had a helicopter hovering overhead with the flood light and infrared cameras going and this guy still got away Scott free."

"That's incredible," Steven says. Then he thinks a moment then and changes the subject.

"Hey Alex, do you know of any places that are looking for construction workers right now or sometime in the near future?"

"No, can't say that I do. You're not working?"

"The company where I was working slowed down. They laid me off Thursday."

"Oh dude. I'm sorry to hear that. Man, I wish I

could tell you I knew who's hiring. But the ugly truth is, nobodies is."

"That's OK, I just thought I'd ask."

"How does Vicky feel about you being out of work right now?"

"She doesn't know. I haven't told her. Didn't want to spoil everyone's weekend."

"Yeah I hear you. Listen, I'll keep asking around. And if anything comes up I'll call you, OK. Just hang in there pal. I'm sure the good Lord will deliver. Just you watch."

*

In a different part of the church Vicky's talking with Steven's mother, Amy amongst other church visitors. "...well if you need any help around the house," Vicky says, "Don't hesitate to give us a call. That's what family's for."

"I'm doing all right. Just keep praying for me. Where are the boys? I haven't seen my two grandsons today. Did they come?" Amy asks.

"Sure they're here... probably outside, playing with some of the other kids. You know how boys are."

"Do I. Steven used to be the same way when he was little. Outside running around all the time."

"You know, it's funny you should mention Steven being little. He just had a dream this morning about being little. He woke up all emotional with tears in his eyes."

"Oh my goodness. Was it about his father?"

"No. He said it was about his grandmother."

"Poor thing, he was so close to his grandma. After his father died we would visit with her almost everyday."

"You should've seen him. He was kind of embarrassed and trying not to let me see the tears."

"What was his dream about?"

"He didn't say, exactly... All he said was that he was a little boy again and held her and kept telling her that she was alive. Oh and he remembered smelling toast and bacon."

When Amy hears the phrase "she was alive," it suddenly reminded her of something that happened in the past. Something Grandma Lee told her. She never knew what to make of it. Writing it all off as just a hallucination triggered by a combination of an aging memory and falling behind on her medication or something else. But to hear about it again, now, after all these years. Remembering how frightened Grandma Lee was shaken by it all.

"Amy?" Vicky asks.

Amy looks intently at Vicky.

"Amy... What is it?" Vicky asks, a little more concerned now.

"Vicky, it really happened."

"So it's a memory from his past?"

"No. It couldn't have been."

"But you just said it really happened."

"I know but we never told Steven about it."

"You never told him what? I don't understand. What do you mean you never told him?"

"Listen, we shouldn't talk about this here. Can I come over later?"

"Of coarse. Come over for dinner."

"What time?"

"Is 5 o'clock OK for you?"

"That's fine. We need to talk more about this. Tell Steven I had to run."

"OK. we'll see you later."

Chapter 26

Back in Tina's apartment Joey is sitting at the kitchen table shirtless, smoking a cigarette and playing with the Glock 19. A loaded ammo cartridge is lying on the table next to one of the bullets, a pack of cigarettes, and a half finished bottle of beer. He snaps the bullet into the cartridge, then loads the cartridge, moves the slide action then pretends to aim and shoot an imaginary target. Taking a drink from the beer bottle, he looks at the markings on the gun and notices the serial number partially filed off. He sets the beer down on the table and brings the pistol in for closer inspection. This makes the gun impossible to trace, he thinks. Not knowing much about handguns, he wonders to himself how much he could sell it for. He takes the cartridge out and works the slide action causing the bullet to jump out of the gun and then catches the bullet. Then he sets the gun, and the bullet down next to the cartridge on the table and takes a deep puff from his cigarette.

"Tina!" he calls out.

Tina walks in tiredly sliding in her slippers, wearing an oversized T-shirt, hair still undone, and eyes half closed. She obviously looks as if she just got out of bed and is still half asleep. As if they had a code of their own she reaches out with a sideways peace sign and Joey immediately knows she wants a puff of his cigarette and hands it to her.

"What?" she asks, then takes a puff.

"Make something to eat."

Tina sits at the table, evidently tired not just from working late last night but also from the after party Joey insisted on having when they got home last night. Tina is still upset at Joey for what ever it was he was up to that he insisted she clock out at Lucy's in the middle of her shift just to go pick him up. Then for getting drunk out of his mind and be loud and obnoxious late at night, and causing the neighbors to call apartment security and filing a formal complaint, leaving another bad mark against them.

"Go buy something," she says, "I'm tired."

Then she notices the gun and her eyes widen. If Joey ever had anything to do with guns he's never brought it up in the past let alone bring one to the house. Tina is dead against any kind of guns in her house or in anyone's house if she could have it her way, and just because her boyfriend Joey has one here, that isn't going to soften her hard objections to them. And even more so, after the way he was acting last night.

"Joey, get this crap out of here. I don't want it in my house."

"Just calm down, it ain't even loaded."

"I don't care! I said don't want it here."

"Just calm down, already."

"I mean it, Joey."

"Stop... just shut up."

"Don't you tell me to shut up."

"OK, Fine... Then just calm down."

Tina sits looking away with her arms crossed and takes a puff from the cigarette and extinguishes the butt on a small plate full of butts.

"Look, I'm just hanging on to it till I can find someone to buy it."

"Why don't you let Jeff hold it for you?"

"Jeff's most likely in jail right now."

"He what?... What did you guys do?"

"Why does it have to be my fault? I have nothing to do with him being in jail. He screwed up on his own."

"OK then. What did he do?"

"He got caught with Carl selling dope."

"And where were you when all this happened?"

"I was up the street waiting to meet him at McDonald's, right where you picked me up."

"Where did you get the gun?"

"Carl asked me to hold it for him, while he and Jeff go take care of their thing. How was I supposed to know they were going to a drug deal?"

"Well you did the right thing by not going with them. Who knows, you might be in jail too."

"Thank you. Lucky for them they didn't have the gun with them when they got caught. They would have been in even bigger touble. Maybe I can sell this gun and we'll have some extra cash, hell, you know we could always use some extra cash."

Tina picks up the 9 millimeter bullet and looks closely at it. Thinking about how something so small can kill a person. Then she wonders if maybe one day this very bullet in her hand could be the death of someone. She puts the bullet back down on the table.

"Joey, why don't you just throw it away?"

"Are you crazy? That's a stupid idea. I bet I can get at least $300 for it. I'll keep $100, give $200 to Carl's cousin, and tell him that's all I could get for it. He won't want this gun at his place right now. Carl's in jail, so he's probably trying to lay low on a count of the cops are probably watching him now."

"Joey just be careful. I don't want you getting caught in the middle of something stupid."

Joey sets the gun on the table and gets up and takes the T-shirt from the back of the chair he was sitting on, puts it on and starts for the front door.

"Where are you going?" Tina asks.

"I'm going to get something to eat."

"Well don't leave this gun here on the table!"

Joey lets out a sigh to express his irritation at the inconvenience and picks up the bullet snaps it into the cartridge, then picks up the gun and places them all in the small paper bag, rolls it up and places it in a cabinet above the refrigerator and leaves through the front door.

Chapter 27

It's after 5 o'clock now and back at Steven's house, he and the boys are watching "The Dead Zone" an old Steven King movie on TV, while Vicky and Amy are in the kitchen. Amy's sitting at the table having a cup of coffee, as Vicky is pours herself and cup adds cream and sugar.

"In his dream. How old was he? Amy asks."

I" don't remember. I don't think he mentioned it. Only that he was a little boy. Why?"

"I thought I'd long forgot about it. But when you said those words, "she's alive," it all came back to me as if it just happened yesterday."

"Amy, what do you mean? What happened?"

"A long time ago, the same year that Steven's dad died, we were visiting my mom. I think it was a Saturday morning..."

*

1984

Steven vanishes in Grandma Lees arms. Resisting the instinct to scream, she gets a chill, frightened by what just happened. Then the front door visible from where she's standing opens.

"Oh my god!," she gasps.

Amy walks in carrying a bag of prescription medicine but doesn't hear Grandma Lee gasp as she's complaining about the customer service at the store.

"Sorry we took so long... they really should hire more people at that stupid store, their so darn slow..."

Then Amy notices the look of terror on Grandma Lee's face and frightened that she might be experiencing some medical emergency she expresses her concern.

"Mom?... Are you OK?"

Grandma Lee braces herself on the kitchen counter top as if maintaining her balance and watches in a state of horror as Steven walks in the front door licking the ice cream cone and immediately stops when he notices the cartoons playing on TV, and sits on the floor getting comfortable to watch TV. Amy hurries to Grandma Lee's side and when she realizes her distress has something to do with Steven her concern grows a little curious.

"Mom! What's the matter?!"

Still in shaking nervously in a state of shock and speechless, Grandma Lee holds onto Amy as she walks her to the nearest chair at the dining room table and sits down. Grandma Lee still hasn't taken her eyes off of Steven who's still engaged with the Saturday morning cartoons playing on the TV.

*

"She never told me what happened that day," Amy says, "Not till a couple of days before she passed away. She told me it was really Steven who visited her. Not a ghost or a spirit of some kind. She really believed it was him. I thought to myself, "this is crazy talk". I didn't dare tell her that. And I never told anyone else about it, not even Steven. Never saw any reason to. He was only 9 years old. I thought I'd forgotten about it, till you told me today of his dream. Even the fact that you mentioned the smell of toast and bacon in the house. I remembered too, that when I walked in the house, it smelt like bacon and toast. I was going to say something about that but I was busy blabbering about the slow service at the drug store, then I saw the look on her face. Funny thing is I completely forgot about the bacon and toast smell till you brought it up today."

"So if I ask Steven what age he was in his dream and he says 9... What do you think it means?" Vicky asks.

"I don't know. But after you told me of his dream, I felt like I really needed to tell you about what happened that day. I don't know how it could be possible for Steven to have known anything about it. When Grandma Lee told me she said she never told anyone else about it. And I never did either."

*

Later that same night.
Grandma Amy has already went home for the night. Steven is sitting in the den at a folding leg card table spreading out puzzle pieces and turning some over. The boys are in the living room playing a video game on TV, and Vicky walks in with a bowl of fresh popped popcorn and a soda.

"This was a good idea, Vicky. What made you think to buy this puzzle?"

Vicky sits next to Steven and sets the bowl on the table. Steven takes a couple of kernels and pops them in his mouth.

"I don't know. I just saw it there, and I thought it would be fun for all of us to work on."

She sits, and they both look down and begin the 1,000 piece puzzle challenge. Then she hears the boys cheer from the living room about their latest achievement on their video game. She starts to get up to go tell them to come and help with the jigsaw puzzle but Steven touches her arm to stop her.

"Let them play their game. I think we can handle this on our own."

Vicky smiles, and sits back down.

"OK, Sure... We can do this."

They work together on the puzzle and she casually brings it up Steven's dream from this morning.

"Hey, in that dream you had this morning about your grandma? How old were you in it?"

"Oh Gee, I'm surprised you even remembered I told you about it. Ah I don't know, about 9. Why?"

Vicky let's out a gasp, that turns into a nervous smile.

"Oh my god."

"What, am I missing something here?"

"Well, your mom and I were talking after dinner, and she said when you were 9 something very similar to your dream happened to your grandma."

"She had the same dream?"

"No silly. Your mom said she saw you... As a ghost."

"My mom saw me as a ghost?"

"No... Your mom said your grandma saw you as a ghost."

"Really? Me as a ghost?"

"She said you were real at first. Then you disappeared in her arms. Like a ghost. Oh, and you were saying "Grandma, your alive" over and over."

"I don't remember disappearing in my dream, but then again I was in her arms then I woke up."

"Steven, this is crazy. First the house is being haunted, then this dream you have... Do you think maybe your grandma is trying to contact you from the other side or something?"

"No... I don't think so. To begin with. If she's gonna make contact with someone, why not choose someone who believes in that sort of stuff?"

"Like Aunt Marie? That would make more sense. Don't you think?"

"I don't know. Maybe she chose you, to make a believer out of you."

"I don't think so."

"Why not?"

"Well... in my dream, I don't remember her giving me any important messages or special advice or anything. She just asked me if I wanted a snack or a sandwich or something."

"Well just think about this for a moment... Maybe there's a message in there somewhere?"

"Honestly I don't think so. Did you ever think that maybe you're over thinking this?"

"What else did she say?"

"That's all, she just asked me, was if I wanted something to eat. I answered yes, but once I realized that she was alive and back from the dead, all I could think of was how happy I was to see her. She didn't tell me anything I didn't already know. Vicky, it was just a dream. People dream stuff like that all the time. And as for what you said a minute ago about this house being haunted, forget about it. It's over now. It's been two days since anything unusual has happened. I think the ghost or whatever it is took the hint that we're not gonna be intimidated."

"Steven I hope you're right about all this."

Vicky goes back to working on the puzzle then she remembers that tomorrows Monday.

"Where are you working tomorrow?"

"No work tomorrow," Steven says without looking up from the puzzle.

Vicky stops working on the puzzle and looks at Steven.

"No work tomorrow either?"

"No... Actually, I may be off for a month or two... maybe longer, I don't know."

"How long have you known?"

"Known?"

"How long have you known you were laid off?"

"Since Thursday."

"When were you planning to tell me?... Is that what you and Alex were talking about today?"

"John said it was only a temporary slowdown and when things pick up they'll call me back. As far as me talking with Alex this morning, I was just putting a little feeler out there to see how the immediate job market is. If anyone knows of a job out there, it would be him. Beside that I didn't want to spoil our weekend."

"What did Alex say?"

"He said he'd call me if he knew of any jobs."

"Does he know anyone who's looking to hire right now?"

"No, he said right now jobs are scarce."

"Listen to me you jerk. You need to tell me when you get laid off or about other things like that. We're partners, aren't we? This affects all of us. Besides, how do you know I can't help you find a job? I have friends, maybe they might know of a job opening out there for you."

"Really?... You know of a job out there waiting for me?"

"No... Of course I don't. I didn't even know you needed a job until a minute ago. But I can still help you look for work, right? I love you, you big dummy. And we need to share the hard times as well as the good. Remember what the pastor said in church today? Share each others burdens, and don't think there's any shame when others offer to help you to carry your cross."

She plants Steven a big kiss.

"Love you," he says.

Vicky laughs nervously and wipes tears from her eyes.

"Love you too, you big lug. Cheese"

"Crackers."

"One makes the other that much better."

They hug.

"Let's go to bed," Vicky says.

Vicky stands up and starts to leave.

"What about the puzzle?"

"We've done enough for now. We can do more tomorrow. It isn't going anywhere."

"What do you mean, we only did about 20 pieces."

"Well, you can go ahead and try to finish. I got work in the morning. So don't try and wake me if you come in and find me sleeping."

Steven thinks a second looking at the puzzle then he gets up takes the bowl of popcorn and follows Vicky out of the den turning the light out at the door.

Chapter 28

**Monday,
2:00 am.**

Vicky gets up from bed tired and half asleep, awakened in the middle of the night to answer natures call. Walking from the bathroom up the dark hall to and into the kitchen for a cup of water to sate a sudden onset of late night thirst she notices light coming from the direction of the living room. She goes to the living room and it becomes more evident that the light is actually spilling out from the partially open door to the den. The horrifying thought of the ghost returning enters her mind and not wanting to disturb Steven from his sleep she nervously but quietly braves her way forward hoping it's just one of the boys. She pauses to let her courage build a little further and prepares to give whoever she finds a hushed scolding for being awake so late on a night before school. At the doorway to the den which is partly opened she slowly opens it all the way and to her surprise she see's Steven fully dressed and holding a piece of the jigsaw puzzle with a quizzical look on his face.

"I never even heard you get up. How long have you been out here?" she asks.

"Oh, hi. Not long. This puzzle isn't so hard."

She sees the puzzle more than 1/4 complete. And her eyes widen.

"Oh my goodness. You're gonna finish it in one night."

Steven doesn't say anything more as he looks at the completed portion of the puzzle still holding the same puzzle piece in his hand.

"Don't stay up all night," she says as she leaves the room.

Vicky walks back into the dark bedroom and slides in bed, and immediately feels someone in bed next to her. Immediately startled and frightened, she jumps out of bed and screams, thinking that the ghost has chosen to make it's presence known here in the privacy of her own bed. But instead of a ghost haunting her bedroom a man is awaken from his sleep in her bed.

"What?!... What's the matter?!" he says.

She immediately recognizes Steven's voice and turns on the light, to reveal that in fact it is Steven.

"How, how did you get in here?"

"What's the matter with you? This is where I sleep."

"Steven, you were in the den fully dressed and working on the puzzle just now!"

"Did you have a bad dream?"

"Oh my god, Steven!! I just came from there! I saw you! Come on, get up, you need to see this!"

They both get up and walk to the den, where the

light is still on. Vicky knows she wasn't dreaming. And she knows it was Steven she just spoke to. When they get to the den there's nobody there.

"Oh my God, Steven, I saw you. Sitting right here. You were working on the puzzle. Look! Look at how much is done!"

The card table still set up as they had left it, with the puzzle pieces scattered, except now over 250 pieces are assembled, confirming Vicky's story that someone was in here working on the puzzle.

"Vicky, I was sleeping all this time. There's no way I could have did this."

Chapter 29

Later still into the same night.

Steven is in bed sound asleep and he starts dreaming.

His dream places him in the business district part of town where he's casually walking up the sidewalk unconcerned about what he's doing here or where he's going at the moment. As if he were on automatic pilot, he turns and walks into an auto body shop.

The manager is sitting in his office at a desk looking at a Hotrod magazine when he notices what he believes to be a customer walking in through the front door. He tosses the magazine aside and steps out of his office and to the front counter.

"Hi, Can I help you, buddy?"

Still on auto-pilot the unrehearsed words come out of Stevens mouth, "Hi, I'm looking for a job. Are you guys doing any hiring right now?"

What went from a paying customer to another reminder of how business has gone bad during the past couple of years, the manager says, "Sorry pal, just laid half my crew off last month."

"OK. Thank you," Steven says, somewhat robotic and unconcerned. Pausing briefly, he notices a Coca-Cola clock hanging on the wall behind the counter. It strikes him as odd that a clock like that would be in a body shop. That's the kind of clock you would expect to see in a fast food diner or a snack bar. Not here in an auto body shop. Then he turns around and walks back out the front door, still on auto pilot.

Once outside the front door he catches a whiff of the hotdogs steaming in a vending cart not far away. Steven stands for a moment wondering what it is he's supposed to do next. He turns to his right and walks in that direction for no particular reason. Up ahead he sees the sidewalk hot dog vendor (an older man in his late 60's), selling hot dogs, chips, pretzels and soda. A couple of young punks wearing hoodie's and baggy jeans are trying to intimidate the vendor to persuade him to give them a free meal, but the vendor is holding his ground and nervously refusing. As Steven gets closer he's able to make out what the two thugs are saying.

"Yo, come on old man, give us a bite. It ain't gonna set you back, dog!"

Dude, we're your protection here. We're the only reason you don't get jacked and shut down, dog. Give us a bite, chump. Don't make us hurt you.

Steven continues walking towards them and the bully's are taking notice. Steven reaches the hot dog cart and one of the thugs immediately doesn't like Steven being there and voices his discontent.

"Yo, yo, yo, dog...mind your own business. You don't belong here. You need to just keep moving along."

Steven realizes now that he's in a dream. And there's no way these guys are gonna hurt him. In fact maybe he can even have a little fun here.

"I'm just here to have myself a hot dog," Steven says.

The first thug pulls out a switch blade and
wields it, trying to intimidate Steven. But Steven isn't
phased. This is his dream, and in his dream he
makes the rules. And rule number one, he's the hero.
The bully takes the knife tries to stick Steven in the
gut, but Steven parry's the jab with a lightning fast
deflector block. Then Steven turns his back to the
thug and grabs the guys hand and with a nerve pinch
he easily separates it from the knife as the thug
winces in pain. Then Steven takes the knife and
closes the switch blade and pockets it, as the other
thug gets behind him and hits him on top of the head
with a small baton, but it has no effect, he kicks the
first bully in the groin causing him to double over.
Then bully that hit on the head start's to follow up
with a punch to Steven jaw but Steven blocks the
punch quicker than can be seen and counters with
three lightning fast jabs to the thugs face, causing
him to immediately get a nose bleed and pass out
right on the spot. The thug on his knees doubled over
from the groin kick looks up at Steven who turns
around and pulls out the switchblade and hands it to
the thug. "You really shouldn't be playing with
knives," Steven says. And turns his back as if to walk
away.

The thug gets up from his knees and snaps open
the blade again and attacks Steven from behind.
Steven hears the switchblade snap open and quickly
responds by stepping to his right and turning
sideways just as the thug thrusts the blade forward
into where Steven was just a millisecond ago. Steven
upper cuts the mans hand holding the switchblade
which is caught by surprise and lets the knife go
which flings upward and sticks into a faux plaster
cornice up above the second floor high out of reach

near the roof edge of the building. With one punch Steven knocks him out cold. Then he drags both of them by their shirts, away from the vendor and leaves them lying asleep, next to a trash dumpster.

As Steven walks back, passing the vendor, continuing toward the corner, he glances upward and sees the switchblade stuck high out of reach in the buildings cornice. Then Steven looks over at the hot dog cart and smiles and nods a friendly gesture at the vendor who's stunned and not quite sure what it is he's has just witnessed.

The vendor looks back at the two bully's laying on the ground, then back at Steven, but he's gone. He's confused about where Steven may have gone. He wasn't close enough to the corner to make the turn, nor were there any alley ways or doors that he could have ducked into. His sudden disappearance has him confused. He was quick with his moves when he dealt with the two thugs but how could he just vanish in thin air.

*

Stevens dream instantly places him back at home in the den. He's sitting at the fold out card table working on the puzzle. He selects a puzzle piece at random and places it in its proper position. Then another and another. As if he were once again on auto-pilot, Steven makes remarkable progress picking pieces at random and locating every piece he picks up in it's proper place. Even pieces that don't interlock with the built section he is able to drop them in place and within the next two or three pieces he finds the pieces that chain them together. In less than a couple of minutes he has assembled more than a quarter of the puzzle. Then suddenly as if writers block has set in, the luck of the draw that allowed him to select over two hundred and fifty correct puzzle pieces in a row gives out and in his hand he holds a piece that doesn't seem to fit anywhere within the two or three piece degree of separation. The assembled portion of the puzzle rests in front of him awaiting his next move.

Then Vicky appears at the doorway in her nightgown.

"I never even heard you get up. How long have you been out here," she says.

"Oh, hi. Not long. This puzzle isn't so hard," Steven responds still wondering what happened that suddenly caused his luck to run out.

Vicky sees the puzzle about 1/4 complete. And her eyes widen.

"Oh my goodness. You're gonna finish it in one night."

Steven doesn't respond as he looks at the completed portion of the puzzle still holding the same puzzle piece in his hand.

"Don't stay up all night," She says as she turns and heads back to the bedroom.

Still looking down at the puzzle Steven looks at the piece he's holding and back at the finished portion of the puzzle. Why did it stop? Over two hundred and thirty pieces in a row. What are the odds? Is it even possible to randomly select that many correct pieces in a row? Looking down at the assembled portion of the puzzle Steven starts to begins to recognizes where he is and what just happened. I know this, he thinks to himself. But from where? Then he remembers. Vicky woke me up in the middle of the night and told me I was here putting this together! And now, here I am! He hears Vicky scream from the bedroom and jumps up quickly and rushes out of the den.

As soon as he leaves the den, the light goes out behind him and he realizes that he's in a dark house. He goes kitchen, turns on the light. Then he quietly walks to the bedroom and sees that the lights are out and it's calm in there as if nothing is wrong whatsoever. He notices the bathroom light on and the door closed so he walks back into the kitchen. He opens a cabinet where he sees some instant cocoa mix and reaches for the tea kettle to heat some water. Then he feels it's empty, so he takes it to the sink to fill it with water. Right before he turns on the water he's startled by Raziel standing next to him.

"Oh my gosh! Raziel. What are you doing here?" Steven sets the tea kettle in the sink.

"Steven, look what you're doing," she says.

Steven looks at the cabinet open and the kettle in the sink.

"What do you mean?" he asks.

"Steven, the tea kettle... don't you remember?"

"Remember what ?" Steven asks, "What are you talking about?"

"Steven you're dream traveling again. It wasn't that long ago."

Steven looks at the tea kettle in the sink and he turns on the water. Then he looks up at the open kitchen cabinets. Then he thinks to himself that if Raziel is here and he sees and recognizes her then he must be dreaming.

"Wait a minute, I remember this..."

Steven dream travels away, everything goes black and this time he sees a quick flash of newspapers scattered on the ground. Then everything goes black again. Then he sees himself on his knees holding his mid section. Then once again everything goes black. Then he sees himself on his knees with a man pointing a gun to his forehead. Then he finds himself at the batting cages standing across from Raziel.

"Steven it's you!"

"What do you mean me? What's me?"

Remember when I told you that your were dream traveling? You're the one who left the lights on, and the tea kettle in the sink. You're haunting your own house.

"But I'm just dreaming all this. Right? It can't be real..."

"Steven this place here isn't real. This place is imaginary. But when you were at home in your kitchen. That was real. When you were working on the puzzle in your den. That was real. And when you beat up those two men. That was real."

"But I thought I was dreaming."

"You are. But your dream took you to real places and real time. Even the dream you had about your grandma being alive. That was real. You were really there with your her. You nearly scared her to death when you vanished in her arms."

"But if I was dreaming, that would mean I'm at home in bed. How can I be somewhere else at the same time?"

"Your body is in bed right now. But you are here in this form. It was also Friday for those guys you beat up. And 26 years ago for your grandma. Steven, your dream took into the future and into the past."

"What about the super strength I had... I mean, I was able to disarm those big thugs who came at me with a knife. I was super quick and when one of them hit me I didn't feel a thing."

"You're not here in your natural human body."

"What does that mean?"

"The limits from your world don't apply to you when your dreaming. You don't feel pain unless you choose to. If you believe that you could move faster than what would be normal. You will. If you choose to allow it, you could hold your breath under water indefinitely."

"Raziel, there's one thing I've been seeing in my dreams that I don't understand."

"Go on."

"It's like I'm dreaming within my dream. I'm seeing flashes of events in broken sequences. In them, I appear to be bleeding like I got stabbed or shot. Then at one point it appears as if I'm about to be executed."

"These dream flashes within your dreams are they memory flash backs?"

"I've never experienced anything like that in my life."

"Then maybe their flash forwards."

Steven feels his body starting to shake uncontrollably. In spite of all the effort Steven makes to stop the shaking, his body continues to shake as if he were being controlled by some unseen force.

"Woe, What's happening to me?"

He looks at Raziel for some explanation as to what is attacking him in this imaginary world.

Raziel looks up and outward as the batting cages also start rattling and all the ground begins to tremble as if a great earthquake were happening, she starts shouting at him, "You're waking up Steven, Steven, wake up!...Steven, wake up!"

Chapter 30

Home in bed, Steven is being vigorously shaken awake by Vicky, who's eyes are full of tears as she shouts, "Steven, wake up! Steven, wake up!"

Steven slowly snaps out of his deep sleep still visibly tired, yet trying to remember all of what he has just dreamed. It seemed to him like his dream had lasted two or three days, yet the dreams he's been experiencing were broken sequences of about 20 minutes divided up through half the night. And the only details he is able to recall of his dream add up to what could only be a few minutes. In town looking for work... fight at the hot dog cart... working on the puzzle... making hot cocoa in the kitchen...the batting cages.

"OK, OK . I'm awake. What's going on?"

"Steven, you weren't breathing!"

Steven forgets about his dream as he notices the seriousness of what Vicky is telling him because she's wiping tears from her face. He tries to calm her down.

"Of coarse I was... I was just sleeping."

"Steven, you weren't breathing. I even checked your pulse, and I couldn't find one!"

Not breathing, no pulse, Seven thinks to himself. I'm ok now though. I just need to calm Vicky down. Take her mind off of what just happened. "What time is it?" he asks.

"Steven! I thought you were dead!!"

"You're serious?" he says trying to play it off.

"Yes! I was getting ready to call 911!"

"You're really serious. You thought I was dead?"

"Stop it, I'm not joking here! This is a very serious matter."

"OK, OK... I'm sorry. I didn't mean to sound condescending. What happened?"

"You're not going to make fun of me?"

"No, I won't do that... So you thought I was dead?"

" At first I thought you were just in a deep sleep. Then I tried to wake you up. I called you a few times. Then I looked at you. And when I didn't see you moving, I felt you to see if you were breathing. I couldn't feel your breath. I couldn't hear your heart beat."

"Really? How long was I like that?"

"I don't know... Steven! I thought you were dead!"

"Well, I'm not dead, as you can see."

"Are you gonna be OK? Maybe I shouldn't go to work today," she says.

"No, I'm fine... Don't worry. You need to go to work. We need your income right now."

If living in a haunted house isn't bad enough now there's the worry that Steven might be drifting into death in his sleep. This is going to be a long day. Or tonight's going to be an even longer night. Frustrated at Steven, Vicky gets out of bed and leaves the room to take her morning shower.

Chapter 31

**Monday,
10:30 a.m.**

Wal-Mart section manager Mikey makes his daily walkthroughs conducting spot checks for any tripping hazards, slipping hazards, items misplaced on shelves and any customers or fellow employees in need of assistance. As he walks through the toy department he's approached by a customer.

"Excuse me," the customer calls to him.

"Yes sir, how can I help you?," Mikey says.

"I've been trying to find Pokemon cards for my nephew... do you guys sell them?"

"Yes sir, let me show you where they are," Mikey says and leads the customer around to the next aisle.

Mikey has been working at this store for more than two and a half years and has the layout of the toy department engraved in his memory. Staying up to date on the latest toy fad, he usually knows what's hot and what's not. He usually knows exactly what the customer is talking about even when they themselves are not sure what it is their kids want.

"There you go sir. Is there anything else I can help you with?"

"No, that's all, thank you."

"No problem. If you need anything else we have an associate working this area, who would be glad to assist you."

"OK, thank you."

Having just committed the employee working this section to assist this customer with assistance from here on, Mikey looks around for Joey who is currently assigned to this section. He sees the basket full of toys halfway down the aisle. Joey brought this basket of toys here to be restocked. But he's not anywhere in the immediate area.

Mikey goes to the next department over, which happens to be the electronics department. He finds Janet working the register, currently checking out a customer.

"Hey, Jan, have you seen Joey?"

"No, not for a while," she says.

"Is he working today?"

"Yea, he was here earlier this morning. I just don't know where he is right now."

"He didn't say where he was going?"

"No sir, not to me. He didn't tell me anything."

Mikey's first instinct is to check the stock shelves in the back of the store. He goes to the back of the store and asks the other employees back there if any of them has seen Joey back there. The only time they say they saw him back there was earlier that morning when he came back there to take a basket full of toys that needed to be shelved out for display. But other than that they haven't seen him all morning. Mikey walked the aisles to see if maybe he was back there anyway and maybe the other employees just didn't see him. He doesn't see him anywhere.

Then Mikey checks the break room. It's not uncommon for employees to suddenly remember they forgot to leave or take something of importance from their locker, or if maybe they just needed to take a sudden break because they're feeling ill. Mikey goes to the break room but doesn't find Joey.

Next Mikey's checks the smoking area out in front of the store. If Joey turns up out in front of the store, having an unauthorized smoke break it's bad news for him. But as it turns out, Joey isn't out in front of the store either.

Mikey makes his way back to the toy department and sees that Joey still hasn't returned to his section of responsibility. He finds Janet again this time she's helping another customer with televisions.

" Excuse me, Janet, have you seen Joey yet?" he asks.

"No, Mikey, still haven't seen him."

The only one place that Mikey hasn't checked and has been hoping he wouldn't have to, is the restroom. It could be possible that Joey has become ill, perhaps a sudden attack of the stomach flu, which is a legitimate reason for an extended toilet visit. Mikey's now harboring mixed feelings. He doesn't want Joey to be sick, but he doesn't want to find out that he's malingering either. If he had to choose between the two, finding him sick would make his job easier but still he might have to call a medical emergency, or the best case scenario would be that he would just send Joey home sick for the rest of the day. He quietly walks into the men's room and he hears Joey in one of the stalls talking loudly on his cell phone.

Chapter 32

11:30 a.m.

Jogging his usual route Steven, is wearing the new dark blue shorts and a gray shirt Vicky bought him. He likes the comfortable loose feel of his new workout clothes and even though his muscles still feel little sore, he feels stronger today, so he kicks his pace up a notch. Turning the corner he notices another jogger ahead of him struggling and moving at a sluggish pace. He also notices the brown shirt and outdated black shorts the guy is wearing and grins as he thinks to himself, "Thank you for the new shorts, Vicky." Effortlessly he passes the other runner and sends out a greeting of encouragement, "Hang in there buddy!"

Up ahead he sees the traffic light and he races to catch a green light at the corner but it turns yellow, then quickly to red before he gets there. So he slows to a stop at the corner and presses the button on the pole as he waits for the green light. Waiting for the light to change he hears the caw of a crow and he notices a the big black bird perched high on a lamppost across the street. Then he hears a car screech to a stop across the street almost hitting a bicycler that had just cut him off. The driver shouts out his window at him, "What's the matter with you!"

He realizes that everything happening from the moment he passed the other jogger to this point has played out exactly like a memory from the past. Easily passing him then racing for the green light that quickly turned yellow to red, the crow, then the real clincher was the commotion between the driver and the bicyclist at the opposite corner. De-ja vu? Why do I remember this?... He wonders. Did this exact thing already happen once before? Preoccupied with the idea that this day is a replay, he watches the scuffle happening across the street, and he barely hears the runner approaching behind him then at the same moment he feels the hand touch his shoulder he hears a familiar shout.

"Hey!"

Steven spins around quickly. But no one is there. He waits confused and looking around for a moment still thinking, I remember this. Then sees the light is green and reluctantly returns to his jogging. As he jogs he continues to try and remember why all this seems so familiar to him. Then he remembers. He dreamed all of this not long ago.

Chapter 33

12:00 p.m.

Returning from his lunch break with a soda cup in hand Joey strolls into the break room and heads straight to the time card machine to punch in, but he doesn't see his time card. Looking behind the other time cards for his own just in case his just got covered up by someone else's he realizes his card is not on the board, and he says, "Hey... What the flunk, who took my time card?"

From the managers office located just a few feet away Mikey hears Joey, and calls out to him.

"It's in here, Joey."

Joey walks into the office.

"Hey, Mikey, you took my time card?"

Mikey spent his own lunch hour contemplating how he was going to take care of Joey's most recent flub-up. He doesn't keep an actual file recording minor screw ups that his employees make now and then. Minor mistakes happen often and even by the most experienced workers. But deliberate deception, malingering and slacking off while fellow employees are earning an honest living can only be tolerated for so long. From his own memory which is fairly easy to go on being that all of his employees other than Joey have performed their duties as expected, he is able to rack up more than enough reasons why he should be fired. Joey's attitude has been such that he's above the job he's been given to do and that Wal-Mart is lucky just to have him working for them especially since he has "better places to be and better things to be doing," as Mikey overheard him saying during his most recent phone call in the bathroom stall.

"Joey, we're letting you go."

"Wha...what do you mean?"

"You've been warned too many times about being on the phone."

"Phone? I wasn't on the phone today."

"Joey, don't lie to me. I heard you myself."

"When?"

"During your long bathroom break."

Joey's been caught red handed, and lying isn't going to get him out of his current jam. So he tries to turn the tables by making himself into the victim in this predicament.

"Oh so now I'm being spied on in the bathroom!"

Mikey isn't taking the bait or opening this situation up to debate on his own work ethics. As far as he's concerned his first instinct was that Joey was slacking off somewhere but when he didn't find him right away worry and concern was starting to set in. When he finally located him in the bathroom chatting on the phone with whoever was on the other end and what he heard only confirmed his original suspicion.

"Nobody's spying on you. You can pick your check up Wednesday, if you don't it'll be mailed to you."

Fired. I've just been fired, Joey thinks to himself. And for what? Using the toilet? This isn't fair. It's not like I got caught stealing. I probably should have stolen something when I had the chance, that way it would have been at least partly worth it. I've been so faithful to this stupid store from day one and this is the way they treat me. They should have been looking to promote me to a position seeing how capable I was. How many employees do they have that are able to multitask their duties by taking care of business on the floor while conducting other business elsewhere on their phone. Who do they think they are? Just who the hell do they think they are? Especially this jerk who they call a manager sitting across from me right now!

"Dude. You guys suck!" Joey says.

Joey stands up deliberately letting his chair fall to the floor behind him and storms out knocking everything down and pushing everybody in his path.

"This place sucks!" he shouts out loud and raising his middle finger at everyone as he makes his way through the store and out the front door.

Chapter 34

1:00 p.m.

Steven is sitting in his car, skimming through the list of job prospects he collected and printed out from the internet, then points to the one he's looking for. He looks through his car window at the auto body shop he's parked in front of and compares the addresses. Then he looks at the building front once again and immediately recognizes it from the dream he had last night. "Funny," he thinks to himself, "what are the odds?" How you could pass by a place a hundred times, never enter the doors, then out of the blue you dream about it, the night before the first time you ever walk into the place. Come to think of it I never had any intentions of coming here to look for a job till this morning when I printed up this list. Maybe dreaming about looking for a job here was a good omen. He shuffles through his papers and pulls out a generic cheat sheet he made for filling out job applications. Then he folds it up and puts it in his pocket.

"Well, here goes nothing," he says, and gets out of his car. Walking briskly towards the auto body shop, he notices the hot dog vendor down the street and it causes him to slow down for a better look. The vendor is parked at the same exact location it was in his dream. Then he stops and looks around for the two thugs, but there's no sign of them anywhere. Just a dream, he thinks to himself.

Steven walks through the front door and through the waiting room and although he's never been in this place before he immediately recognizes it. The plastic chairs and coffee table look the same as they had in his dream. He continues to the front counter noticing that every little detail of the place is exactly the same as in his dream, down to the same magazines on the counter, the car posters on the wall, even the same Coca-Cola clock on the wall which he felt looked out of place, like it should've been in a fast food place instead.

Then a young man comes out from the office to greet Steven, and to his own relief the person Steven sees isn't the same person from his dream. This man is at least 20 years younger and looks nothing like the man from his dream. Steven reaches out for a hand shake and he asks, "Hi are you the manager?"

The young employee reaches to shake Stevens hand.

"Oh, sure. I mean no. I'm not the manager... Hold on... I'll go get him for you." he says. Then he leaves through a side door to the work shop. As Steven waits he looks at the photos of custom cars and wrecked cars pinned to a bulletin board on the wall, before and after photos. He doesn't remember any of the photos from his dream, but then again in his dream he didn't remember noticing the bulletin board.

The manager comes through the door wiping his hands with a rag and Steven extends his hand out to greet him. Instantly Steven recognizes the man. Steven knows he's never been in this store before. Maybe he's seen this man in town, at the mall, a restaurant, gas station, bank, it could've been any number of places. "But how would I know to dream that he works here?," He wonders to himself.

"Hi sir," Steven starts to say but the man cuts him off before he can continue.

"Weren't you just in here last Friday?" the manager says, with a confused look.

"No sir. Not me."

"Yeah. You were. You're looking for work, right?"

"Yes, that's right. May I fill out an application?" Steven says with a small grin.

"I told you Friday, we're not hiring."

"Oh, OK. Well, thank you for your time."

As Steven turns and walks to the exit he hears the manager say, "You know you might want to consider making a checklist so you won't waste your time hitting the same places over again, like this."

Steven walks out and pauses on the sidewalk a little confused and wondering for a moment. He remembers dreaming last night that he was here looking for work. Last night. Not Friday, like the manager inside had suggested. "I was here last Friday?," He wonders. In my dream I told myself that I was dream traveling... But it was still just a dream. It was all made up. I just dreamed it all. It wasn't real... or was it.

Steven walks towards his car parked at the curb. When he gets noticed by the sidewalk hot dog vendor, an older man in his late 60's, less than half a block away. The same man from his dream. "Mr.! Hey, Mr.! Over here. Come here!" The man shouts to Steven. Steven sees that it's the same old man from his dream. He gives him a shy wave and replies, "No thanks, I'm OK."

The man's holding up a wrapped hot dog and showing it to Steven and shouting, "No, Mr. , wait!"

Then the man takes the hot dog and grabs a bag of potato chips and runs over to Steven, who just got in his car. Then he taps on the passenger window and signals Steven to roll it down.

"Mr., please." he calls to Steven.

Steven leans over to the passenger side and rolls down the window.

"Sorry, I don't have any money," he tells him.

The man reaches in and hands Steven the hot dog and chips.

"It's free for you. Take it please."

"What? But why?"

"Listen to this guy. You handled those thugs like they were toddlers, last Friday. Those idiots won't come back here again. You're just like a superman. Those guys won't bother me no more."

As the man walks away, Steven sits confused and says to himself, "Did it really happen?"

Steven starts up his car and starts driving and as he approaches the hot dog cart, he slows down to thank the man for the hot dog and chips he just gave him. Through the passenger window that is still rolled down Steven calls out to the man working the food cart, "Excuse me, sir."

Happily the man answers Steven, "Yes sir?"

"I just wanted to say thank you," Steven begins to say then he sees the building behind him and follows the front design upward and high above up above the second floor out of reach he sees the faux cornice. Protruding from the lower part of it he sees the handle of a switchblade knife, stuck in the same spot he dreamed he had flung it.

Chapter 35

1:45 p.m.

Steven walks in the front door with his applications and resumes in a folder. He goes into the kitchen, sets them on the kitchen table then opens the refrigerator and pulls out a bottled water. Then his cell phone rings. Before answering he looks at his caller ID and sees that it's Vicky calling.

"Hi, honey."

"Congratulations you're our one millionth caller!, Vicky says.

"Vicky, you called me."

"Oh yea, that's right. I guess I didn't think this one through very well. Anyway, Hi, honey, I just called to ask you a small favor."

"No problem. What do you need?"

"Could you take the ground beef out of the freezer to thaw. I'm thinking we'll have hamburgers for dinner. You don't mind bar-b-que burgers, do you?"

Steven goes to the fridge, pulls out the ground

beef and sets it in the sink, as he's talking, "Not at all. Sounds great. I'm taking the meat out right now."

"OK, thanks babe. How are you feeling?"

"I'm fine. I went jogging earlier, then went to check out a couple of job prospects."

"Oh, really? How'd it go?"

"It was kind of weird. There's something strange is happening... I'll tell you more about it when you get home."

"Really? You can't tell me now?"

"No, it's kind of a long story. Better to wait until you're home."

"OK then, I'm going to hold you to that and you better tell me the truth... Love you."

"I love you too. Bye."

Steven closes his cell phone as he walks back to the table and looks down at the job applications. Then he hears a loud thud and kind of a crash sound coming from the den, which startles him for a second.

He walks to the den to investigate what caused the noise and when he gets to the doorway he leans in to look first. Scanning the room quickly he doesn't see anyone else in the room but he does see what caused the loud crashing noise. The folding card table with the jigsaw puzzle tipped down on one side with one of the legs folded under. He walks in and lifts the table up and straightens the folded leg. As he sets the table up, the leg that gave out starts to fold back under again revealing the cause of the table falling. It turned out that the hinge lock to that particular leg wasn't engaged. Securing it so it doesn't fall again, he picks up the puzzle pieces and the box off the floor.

Chapter 36

2:00 p.m.

Sitting reclined on a plastic lawn chair in the back patio of the small one bedroom apartment, Joey smokes a joint, while holding a beer can in his other hand. Tina is standing in the kitchen dressed in tight jeans and a halter top, leaning on the door jam with the sliding door open and looking down at him. Coming home early from work in a bad mood, Tina didn't even have to ask Joey to know that he didn't have a job anymore. She was expecting him to quit working there sooner or later anyway, just by the frequency of how much he complained that he hated working there. He told her the reason he lost his job was because two other employees snitched him out for stealing, which he wasn't. Basically he was wrongfully accused of stealing, and it was his word against the word of two other employees who were probably the ones doing the stealing.

"So what are you gonna do?" Tina asks him.

"Guess I gotta go look for another job," Joey says.

"Are you going to apply for unemployment?"

"They fired me, Tina. Don't you get it? You can't get unemployment if you get fired... What are you a moron? Gees, you're so stupid sometimes."

Joey takes a hit from the rolled joint. Tina, upset that Joey just called her a moron and stupid, lashes back at him, "You don't have to talk to me like that, Joey. It's not my fault you got fired... I feel totally bad about you losing your job and all, you know. It's just that I thought I heard once, that if you get fired wrongfully like that or something, the unemployment office can get you your job back. And you could even be paid for lost wages on account that it wasn't your fault."

Pretty sure he doesn't have a case to back him up as far as trying to get his job back Joey changes the direction of the talk. "I don't even want that stupid job back... Those people suck... I can find a better job."

"Yea. Well don't take too long. We still gotta pay bills, you know. Let's go get something to eat before I have to go to work."

"Where do you want to go?"

"Can we try the new burger place by the carwash."

"Yeah, let's go eat," Joey says as he stands up takes a last hit, extinguishes the joint and puts it in an empty breath mint tin where he saves unfinished roaches and walks in and sets it on the kitchen counter. Then he reaches up and opens the cabinet above the refrigerator and pulls out the paper bag with the gun in it.

"Are you bringing that?"

"Yeah, why?"

"Why do you need to bring it?"

"Tina, don't give me any flack right now. I'm not in the mood for this."

"More the reason why you shouldn't be carrying the gun around."

"I'm not carrying it around. It's going to stay in the car."

"Then why even bring it?"

"If I get a call from someone who wants to buy it, I don't want to have to drive all the way back home just to pick it up. This way it'll be gone and out of your precious house sooner. Making us some money and making you happy at the same time."

"What if a cop sees us with it?"

"Like I said, it stays tucked under the seat in the car till we find a buyer. If by some fat chance a cop pulls us over, he'll need a warrant to search the car. Cops don't drive around town with warrants up their butt just waiting for the guy they want to search to drive by. They have to get a judge to sign a warrant before they can use it. And a judge won't sign one without probable cause. You need to watch Law and Order more often. And beside that, it isn't even loaded. If they do find the gun, so what. They find an unloaded gun. That doesn't prove I was going to use it on anybody. It's as dangerous as a crowbar. And there's nothing illegal about having a crowbar in your car."

"I still don't like it Joey."

"Fine, don't like it. You worry too much. Just do me a favor and keep your mouth shut till I sell this thing."

"You shut up."

Joey fakes like he's going to backhand slap Tina, and they both walk out the front door.

Chapter 37

2:45 p.m.

Steven's at home sitting on the couch having fell asleep with the TV playing, he drifts into a dream.

Not a breeze in the calm of night his dream takes him to the batting cage where he swings away at pitch after pitch making perfect contact as usual. Then something different happens. Something that hasn't happened since he was nine years old. The ball whooshes past as him as he swings and misses. Not a splinter of the bat even skims the ball and it slams into the fence at the back of the cage and bounces to a rolling stop on the ground by where he's standing. Strange, Steven thinks to himself, that's never happened before. From the first time he ever dreamed of being here back when he was a child, he hasn't missed a single pitch. As if it had a mind of it's own, the pitching machine waits with it's wheels spinning but obediently holding off it's next pitch as if it were waiting for Steven to ready himself. He stands looking at his bat as if something were wrong with it. I've never missed one before, he thinks, not in my dreams anyway.

Steven doesn't notice that Raziel was standing directly across from him just on the other side of the batting cage. Startling him, she says, "It's not as easy when you start thinking it's real, is it."

"Oh, hi Raziel. What do you mean?"

"When you start believing it's real, your subconscious doesn't give you total perfection. Maybe that's why you missed the ball just now. Don't confuse this place for what's real, Steven."

Steven positions himself to hit and the machine delivers. Steven makes perfect contact sending the ball back as fast as it was pitched up and over the pitching machine then it shuts down.

"Raziel... Why am I dream traveling?" he asks.

"You're only traveling to where you already have been, or where you will be," she tells him.

"But why?"

"Some of the traveling you've done so far seems to have been happening just to convince you that it's really happening. Some of the places you went to was to help others somehow."

"So I'm convinced. But how am I helping anyone?"

The batting cage and the surroundings are instantly changed into a baby blue painted room as Steve dream travels into the past. The room he's in is his own baby nursery back in the year 1975. He didn't notice before but he's wearing a light blue dress shirt and dark pants. Standing at the head of a baby crib he doesn't yet know where he is but he's trying to figure it out. Baby Steven is in the crib having just plopped down on his butt with an open bag of balloons in his tiny hands. Raziel looks around the room admiring the Noah's ark painted animals on the wall. Then she looks at the baby. Baby Steven pulls a balloon out and start to put it in his mouth. But before it happens big Steven reaches in from behind and makes the switch on him, the teething toy for the balloon.

"Oh, no you don't little guy. You shouldn't play with these," he says.

Then he takes out the bag and puts the in the top drawer of the dresser and closes it, and now he recognizes the room. "Hey... This is my old room, back when I was just a kid... But I don't remember all this baby stuff."

"I don't think you were old enough to remember," Raziel says.

"Who's the baby?" Steven asks.

Without giving Steven an answer, Raziel smiles at baby Steven who smiles back at her. "He kind of looks like you," she says, giving him a chance to figure it on his own.

Steven moves around the crib so he can see the baby's face. And just as he makes eye contact with baby Steven, everything changes again just as instantly as it did back at the batting cages. He's now in a convenient store, where he's standing holding his hands up looking at the clerk, who is also with his hands up and very frightened. The clerk not frightened by Steven having just appeared, but by something else that has just happened.

Still confused about where he is now, Steven notices that Raziel isn't here. He's not sure how or why he knows it, but Steven knows that a robbery has just taken place as he and the clerk both start lowering there arms. Then there's a loud startling gunshot from just outside. The clerk ducks down and Steven's reacts by looking to his left towards the front door, and he makes a dash for the front door looking down he notices the newspapers scattered on the floor. He takes care so as not to slip on them as he makes his way to the door. Then pushing the door open he goes through, stops and sees the Circle K sign out at the corner, then he turns immediately to his left but before he can see what the cause of the gunshot was, he dream travels away and finds himself back home sitting on his living room couch.

The commotion and the adrenalin rush he just had less than a second ago fades as he sits trying to figure what it was he was going to see out in front of the Circle K store. He notices the TV isn't on now, it's day light outside, and Raziel is not with him here either... "Wait a minute," he thinks, "I thought I wouldn't be able to remember her. But I do. How is that possible?"

Steven walks slowly toward the dining room, still contemplating how it could be possible that he remembers Raziel. She once told him that he would never know of her existence outside of his dream world. And yet here he is thinking of her. He knows her name, what she looks like and also the fact that she's an angel. Could it be possible that finally after all these years, he just broke the barrier? Or does this mean Raziel herself is crossing the barrier from his dream world and into real life? Then it dawns on him why he's able to recall her in his thoughts. "I'm still dreaming," he says.

Then at that very moment he hears someone trying to open the locked front door frantically. He hears what sounds like a key sliding into the lock and in a state of panic he runs to the door and presses his body against it to keep it from opening.

Who ever it is on the other side is pushing hard trying to gain entry as Steven holds the door from the inside with all his might. Then the intruder eases up for a moment and Steven simultaneously stops pushing from the inside, then he starts to close the door and the intruder outside stops the door and the struggle is on again. Now he hears the person shouting from the other side. Not only is the voice he hears familiar, but he immediately recognizes the spoken words. "Whoever you are, you're busted!!... You're not getting away man!!!"

Steven recognizes his own voice and remembers it was himself on the other side trying to get in. Friday, after I got home from jogging, I sat on the porch and I saw someone walking inside and I was on the outside pushing to get in, he remembers. Steven steps back and lets the door swing open.

Waiting to catch a look at what he knows will be himself coming through the front door, everything suddenly flashes out, as Steven's dream ends and he wakes up.

*

Waking up sitting on the couch, the commotion at the front door is no more. And again the stress he was going through less than a second ago fades. He notices it's not quiet in here this time as he hears a car insurance commercial playing on the TV.

The front door opens and in walks Teddy with his school back pack, followed by Erick, then Vicky, who's carrying what appears to be a store bought apple pie.

"Hi, dad," Teddy and Eric say as they walk in.

"Hi, guys," Steven says, still in the process of waking up, thinking about the dream he just had.

"Hi, honey. Were you sleeping?" Vicky asks him as she closes the front door.

Snapping out of his train of thought and back to reality, Steven says, "Hi... Oh, yea. I don't know, I guess I was just taking a nap. How was your day?"

"It was fine, she says, "I picked up an apple pie for desert."

Chapter 38

When Tina's friend Christina Lawrence turned 19, instead of receiving a nice gift or a night out to dinner from her boyfriend Tony, all she got was phone call from his new girlfriend telling her that he doesn't want anything to do with her anymore and to lose his phone number and not bother him anymore because he and her are together now and she is just a whore from his past that he wants nothing to do with anymore. She didn't do anything to cause this relationship to end. In fact she thought everything was going great. It just turned out that he really wasn't interested in staying with one girl and breaking up wasn't one of his better skills. To make matters worse when she called Tony to find out if this were just a joke he was playing on her, his new girlfriend answered the phone confirming that she was with him and then put him on the phone to tell her himself. He was cold and heartless calling her every name in the book and laughing at her in her in her most depressing moment.

Heart torn in two by the one she loved, Christina cried on and off for over two weeks before she came to the conclusion that he wasn't worth it. From this point on she vowed to never let herself be fooled into believing there would be a man out there that could be trusted. Men are pigs. Now rather than be the one on the losing end of a relationship, she would be the one doing the loving and leaving. She would do the picking and choosing who her men would be, only to temporary fill a void till she deemed it necessary to replace him with by another. Doesn't matter if the other person has a girlfriend or a wife. In fact a wife on the other end would make the guy a great blackmail target. Right now the guy is Joey.

She and Joey connected at a party one evening about three weeks ago and have been seeing each other behind Tina's back since. Christina is a friend of Tina's, but that doesn't take Joey off the playing field. He's just as much a scumbag as any other guy out there. The fact that he's willing to cheat on his girlfriend with one of her friends make him even worse. When the time is right Tina will find out what kind of cheater this Joey guy is and that'll put their relationship to the ultimate test. If Tina decides to stay with Joey, she deserves to be with the cheat garbage he is. If not, then she deserves better. Either way she gets what she deserves, and Christina gets to have fun and a nice gift or some extra cash now and then.

After Joey dropped Tina off at work earlier this evening, he made a bee line to Christina's house as he has every other night since the night they connected at that party three weeks ago. He's been with her all evening. It's about 11:30 pm now, and he's on the front porch talking on his cell phone. Christina is sitting intimately close, almost in his lap with her arms wrapped around him. It's a part of a method that she learned from the lyrics of the song "Wrapped Around Your Finger" by the Police. Shower the guy with phony love and affection, getting him addicted to her. Then dropping him like a rock when the time is right. Sweet revenge never felt better.

"No, I said it's a 9 millimeter glock 19. Totally untraceable." Joey says to the person on the other end of the call.

"How do you know it's untraceable?" the voice on the other end asks.

"How do I know?... Because the serial numbers are filed off."

"What I really want to know is, has it ever been used in a hit?"

"No dude, not even."

"How can you be so sure?"

"Because if it had been, I wouldn't be trying to sell it. I'd be trying to destroy it. Look dude, I'm telling you this gun is clean."

"$300, huh?"

"That's right $300 and it's yours, you can do what you want with it. Just don't try and bring it back."

"How about $150?"

"Don't try to screw me over. The price is $300."

"Alright I'll think about it... and call you back."

"Well don't wait too long, I have other buyers that are interested. It isn't going to last."

Joey slaps his phone shut. Then looks over at Christina and gives her a passionate kiss. Then stops and looks at the clock on his cell phone.

"What time is it?" he asks.

"I don't know." she says.

Seeing that it's already after 11:30, Joey realizes he's running late. "Oh crap! I gotta go! I'm supposed to be at Lucy's now!" he says.

"Aww, Joey why can't I go with you?" Christina says.

"Are you crazy? Tina would kill both of us if she found out."

Chapter 39

Steven home in bed dreaming. In his dream, Vicky, the boys and himself have been window shopping at a nonexistent shopping mall, far more elaborate then any place he's ever been. They come to the food court that has an indoor water park intermingled with a rollercoaster that has cars that ride the rails without making any sound, and multiplex theater projecting previews of feature films out on a huge transparent screen overhead out in the middle of the dining area that can be viewed perfectly from any seat. Steven notices that the ceiling appears to be at least ten stories high and he's in awe. Vicky and the boys don't find anything extraordinary about the place as they find a table sit and discuss what they want to eat.

"I want hot dog on a stick," Teddy says.

"Can I get pizza? Eric asks.

"Steven, honey, what do you think? Do you want

to share a Chinese food combo plate?" Vicky asks.

As Vicky and the boys negotiate what they plan to eat, Steven pulls some cash out of his pocket and at first he sees a large roll of money in his hand. He unrolls it and it amounts to only 3 dollars. Vicky and the boys continue talking back and forth about what food they want, as Steven looks around at all the take out restaurants at the elaborate perimeter décor of the dining area. Then he sees a window to the outside world and his imaginary dream world fades and he finds himself out in the back yard of someone's home where he has just dream traveled to.

It's 1984 now and Steven doesn't realize it but he has just appeared in the real world of a different time and place. Steven looks at the house and the yard and is wondering where he is now. Then he sees Raziel standing right beside him and realizes he's dreaming, but still not sure if this world is real or imaginary.

"Raziel. Where am I?"

"1984," She says.

A faint sound catches Steven's attention.

"Wait, did you hear something?"

"Yes I heard it, for just a second."

The sound happens again and this time it's more recognizable as a dog whimpering.

"Sounds like a small dog in trouble or something."

"It's coming from down there," Raziel says as she points to a vent screen to the bottom of the house.

Steven looks through the screen access panel to the under foundation of the house and he sees a small shadowy figure of what appears to be a small dog, near the middle of the house.

"It looks like he might be trapped in there. We

gotta do something," Steven says.

"It's up to you Steven. There's nothing I can do here except talk to you."

He opens the access panel and crawls towards the dog. About 6 feet into his crawl he hears the distinct sound of a rattle snake and stops frozen from the panic of being within striking range of the aroused venomous predator. Poised upright like a cobra ready to strike at any moment, the snake glares it's fierce round eyes directly at Steven who refuses to look back and make eye contact with it.

Although Steven never saw how Raziel got past him, she is already next to the small dog down on her hands and knees, and she calls out, "Steven!! Why are you stopping? You need to get over here!"

Holding still like a kid caught with his hands in the cookie jar and wishing he could just go back in time, he's trying not to make any moves or sounds that might trigger the snake causing it to strike. Steven whispers, "Raziel. There is a rattle snake looking right at me."

"It won't hurt you Steven," Raziel says, "Get over here. This poor animal needs your help."

Steven slowly moves forward and the snake strikes, lunging forward with its mouth wide open exposing it's long sharp fangs and biting him on the arm. Through his shirt sleeve he feels the pressure of the snakes mouth clamped on his forearm, but doesn't feel any sting from the bite. It feels as if the snake were toothless. He yanks the snake off his arm and throws it aside and it quickly slithers away.

When Steven reaches the trapped dog where it's nearly total darkness, he can hear that the dog is exhausted and from panting in fear. The dog was wearing a leash that had got caught on a nail in a foundation form post that was left anchored deep into the ground back when the house was originally built. Apparently he circled the post, tangling his leash to the point that there was only a few of inches of slack.

"Poor little guy, Steven says, "How long have you been trapped down here."

Steven undoes the collar around the small dogs neck freeing him and he hastily scampers away and out from under the house through a small hole in a vent screen.

Steven crawls out from under the house through the access panel. Then secures it shut. Raziel is already outside, standing close by.

"Steven. You saved this dogs life," she says.

"He's OK for now, but that rattle snake may get him tomorrow."

"Steven the rattlesnake wasn't real. You imagined it."

"What do you mean, not real? I felt it bite me."

"Did you really? Steven, look at your arm," she says.

Steven pushes up his sleeve and looks at his arm and sees that there are no bite marks.

"But I felt it on my arm. I mean I felt it grab my arm. It didn't hurt or anything, but... why did I see it?"

"Let's talk about it later. You probably don't have much time. You should cover the hole that the dog went through so he doesn't get back in there."

Steven goes to the side of the house, finds the hole Skipper went through. Then he finds a large rock that he uses to block the hole in the screen. After satisfying himself that it's secure he stands back next to Raziel and looks at the house. "I know this house," he says quietly, "I used to play out here when I was little. This was my grandma's house. It hasn't changed much."

Just then the dog comes trotting around the corner from the back of the house and when Steven sees him he realizes that the dog is Skipper. So it was Skipper who was stuck under the house. Remembering back to the last time he saw Skipper on a leash, Steven remembers he couldn't get the leash to come undone that day and he just left it attached to the collar and went in the house. Had Steven not been here to rescue Skipper, it's possible he could have died under the house.

Skipper trots casually towards Steven then stops short, sits and looks up at Raziel. Steven takes a knee to pet Skipper. "It's Skipper. Good boy, you don't know how lucky you are that we showed up. Raziel, I think he likes you," he says.

Raziel starts to glow as she starts feeling an unexplainable emotional state. She looks to her left towards the front yard and crouched down by a hedge bush just on the other side of the fence, she sees 9 year old Steven staring right at her.

"Steven I know why you saw me at your grandma's house 26 years ago," she says.

Steven suddenly knows exactly what she's talking about. He realizes that he's wearing the same dark pants and light blue shirt that the man in his grandma's back yard was wearing 26 years ago and he quickly spins around and sees his 9 year old self and as soon as he makes eye contact with the younger Steven, he disappears as he dream travels somewhere else. The day becomes night, and he sees that he is back on the mountain top overlooking the town where he and Raziel once talked 26 years ago.

What ever happened to just dreaming of stuff

that wasn't real, things that didn't matter when you woke up, Steven thinks, Why am I crossing the line intermingling my dreams with reality? Confused and frustrated with how complicated his dreams are becoming Steven says, "Raziel, It's like I'm living a double life. I don't get it. Why is this happening to me?"

"I understand it's difficult for you. But think about what's happening, Steven. From what I've been given to understand, If you didn't steal that silver car a policeman not very far from where you were would have been killed. You saved the old man who was selling hotdogs from a severe life threatening beating. We saw you as a baby, in your crib and you stopped yourself from swallowing that balloon that would have been sure death. Then if it wasn't for you being at your grandma's house in the back yard, poor little Skipper would have surely starved to death."

"So I'm dream traveling to places where I need to help others? Then I disappear?"

"Steven, after you saved the baby's life you didn't disappear until the baby saw you. Then when you rescued Skipper from a death that would've been caused by a mistake you innocently made 26 years ago, it wasn't until you saw your other self that you were dream traveled here. That's what makes you disappear and either wake up or dream travel to a different place."

"My other self?"

"The other you. The baby. The 9 year old Steven. When you made eye contact with them you dream traveled away. Remember?"

"That's right, eye contact... What about that rattlesnake under my grandma's house? Why did I see that?"

"Your subconscious will sometimes allows you to see those illusions. Thoughts or fears that you just might happen to wander into your head. Like the shooting stars in the sky back when we first met. You just thought of them and there they were. But sometimes your own imagination will manifest your worst fears. That's when you need to convince yourself that they are imaginary and you can move right through them."

"How will I know what's real or not?" Steven asks.

"Sometimes it will be easy, and sometimes it won't."

Raziel looks down at the ground and immediately thinks of an idea that might help Steven understand. "Pick up some dirt Steven," she says.

Steven reaches down and scoops up a handful of dirt and notices that there are valuable rare coins mixed within. His eyes widen and shakes his hand sifting the dirt out and leaving only the coins in his hand. "These are gold!" he says excitedly.

"Steven, they're not real," Raziel tells him.

Real or not Steven puts the coins in his pocket for safe keeping just in case they were. Maybe by some miracle he would be able to bring them back to his world with him. Why not? If he, is able to manifest himself in the real world crossing into the past or future then why shouldn't he be able to bring back a simple handful of coins?

Raziel isn't sure what to make of what Steven is trying to do. The coins were supposed to be a simple demonstration of what wasn't real in the dream world. And Steven seems to have fallen for an obvious trick as if she had just told him he has a stain on the chest of his shirt. "Steven, that was supposed to be the easy test," she says.

"I know they're not real... I just want to see something," Steven says.

"Steven, it is important that you recognize what's real. You might feel invincible when you're dreaming, but what you see happening around you could distract you just long enough for something truly disastrous to happen."

Everything changes suddenly as Steven once again dream travels and now he finds himself at home on the front porch without Raziel now.

It's early in the morning, and he is sitting slightly hunched over on the porch bench in front of his house, wearing his exercise clothes now as if he just finished jogging. He thinks about where he notices that he feels a little tired as if he just finished running. Then he rises up from his seat and he goes into the house.

Hanging the keys on the key hook by the kitchen counter, Steven makes his way to the refrigerator where he pulls out the last piece of apple pie left over from last night. He takes the pie in the pie tin, to the kitchen table, sits, takes a bite, chews and swallows. The pie is cold, but it still tastes good, he thinks. And then he takes a moment to ponder about what's going on. Then it dawns on him... the coins! Reaching into his pocket he pulls handful of gold coins out and looks at them carefully, examining the heads and tails sides just before he sets them on the table one at a time. It seems as if his idea to bring the coins with him really worked. "Did I just break a new barrier? Bringing something imaginary into the real world? Raziel never told me I would be able to do this," he wonders. Then he gets up, quickly finds a pad and pen and jots down her name, R-a-z-i-e-l. "I wonder what her name means?" He says quietly to himself.

He didn't notice it before but now he hears the shower running in the bathroom down the hall and then thinks to himself, Vicky's awake, how long has she been in there. Then he hears a man talking to her. He can't quite make out what's being discussed because it's muffled by the closed door and the distance of the bathroom from where he's sitting. Then he hears the shower stop and the bathroom door open and close immediately after. Now he hears the sound of someone coming down the hall. It couldn't be Vicky, the shower just turned off and she would still be in there towel drying. There's no way she would be walking out here wet or naked or even wrapped in a towel. Then he hears a planter in the hall get knocked over, and a mans voice, "Shoot!" "That sounds a little like myself," he thinks as the person he just heard is now picking up the planter that was knocked over. Then he sees himself walk in barefoot wearing shorts and a T-shirt, going straight to the fridge.

Steven now realizes that he must be still dreaming, and sits watching in astonishment as he's looking at himself, not quite sure if he's looking at an event from his past or future. The other Steven didn't notice him sitting quietly at the table as he opens the refrigerator door and starts searching for something. Then the other Steven stops searching the fridge, slowly straightens up, and spins around quickly, seeing himself sitting at the table then makes eye contact, and everything changes suddenly as the Steven sitting at the table dream travels away suddenly finding himself looking out at a Circle K sign from where he's standing out in front of the doors of a convenient store. He's now dressed in the same dark pants and light blue dress shirt he was wearing when he dreamed he was at his grandmas house a while ago. He looks to his left and standing about 15 feet from him is a man wearing a black hoodie with the hood hanging and baggie jeans. The stranger has his back turned to him and is pointing a gun down at the head of another man dressed much like Steven himself, dark trousers and light blue dress shirt. The other man is down on one knee, holding his stomach as if he's been injured. Looking more closely at the man who appears to have just been shot, he notices that the man is someone who looks very much like himself. Steven makes a move towards the man with the gun to try and disarm him. But after taking one step the man down on one knee looks up and Steven and he sees more clearly that it in deed is himself. With the gun pointing right in the face of his other self, Steven makes eye contact and wakes up as he hears a gunshot.

Chapter 40

Tuesday morning.
6:15 am.

Steven wakes up suddenly, alone in bed. Vicky is already up and probably in the shower. Wow, that dream went on, like forever, he thinks. He ponders for a moment, wondering, Did I really just see myself getting killed, or was that imaginary? Why would someone want to kill me? Do I have enemies out there who really want me dead? Or was that just one of those wrong place at the wrong time situations? Thinking back further into his dream, he remembers being at a mall, then Skipper being stuck under his grandmas house. He also remembers being atop of a mountain overlooking the city, then being home eating pie at the table. "Pie, that sound good," he thinks and now he's craving pie. Getting out of bed shirtless and wearing gym shorts, he puts on a T-shirt and goes to the bathroom where, just as he figured Vicky's in the shower. At the bathroom sink, he splashes water on his face then towel dries. Vicky hears him and calls out from the shower, "Steven?"

"Yeah, it's me...Good morning," he says.

"Morning... Steven, you don't know how relieved I am to hear you awake."

"Yea, yea. I know. Was I in deep sleep again?"

"You're scaring me, Steven... This time I could see you were breathing but I gotta admit it looks like your dead. I don't like it. Stop doing that."

"What am I supposed to do? Sleep with a whistle in my mouth? I'll be in the kitchen."

Vicky turns off the shower and Steven leaves the bathroom closing the door behind him. As he walks to the kitchen down the hall, he bumps into a planter and knocks it down. "Shoot!" he grunts in frustration. Then he pick it up back in place.

Continuing into the kitchen, Steven proceeds directly to the refrigerator and opens the door. He didn't notice the figure sitting quietly at the table behind him, as he searches for the pie that was left in there from last night. The one he dreamed of eating earlier. I know we had a piece left over from last night, he thinks. It was here. I know is was right here. I even saw it here in my dream. Thinking of the last time he saw it, he stops. Then he quietly and slowly straightens up. I'm being watched, he's thinking. Spinning around quickly, he sees himself sitting at the table just watching himself at the fridge and immediately makes eye contact with dream traveler Steven who vanishes from the chair he's sitting on. A slice of pie in a pie pan, partially eaten remains on the table. Steven walks nervously, not blinking an eye or looking away from the table as he gets closer to it. The pie sits in the pie tin, with part of it eaten away. No rare gold coins are on the table.

In his dream he had set them right there next to the pie tin, but they're gone now. There is something else on the table that he dreamed of that is here though. The note pad and the pen he wrote on it with. Looking at the pad and pen he can remember writhing on the note pad, but for the life of him he's unable to recall what he was thinking when he wrote the word that he sees written before him now. Raziel.

*

7:00 a.m.

Vicky is now preparing breakfast. Steven is assisting her, but doing more talking than helping, as he tries to convince her of what he just dreamed of and what he just saw a little while ago. Convinced now, more than ever that the house isn't haunted, but instead some kind of unusal remarkable phenomenon is happening.

"Vicky it's me!" he says, "It's not a ghost! At least I don't think I'm a ghost. It's just me! Dreaming!"

"What do you mean, you dreaming?" she asks, as she turns bacon in a frying pan with tongs.

"The person who we're seeing and hearing moving around in the house. It's me! In my dreams!"

"I don't get it. What are you trying to say?... That you're sleepwalking?"

"No nothing like that. But it does happen when I'm asleep. This is something more incredible than that. "

"What do you mean by when you say, it happens?"

"OK. Lets see... how can I explain it? When I'm asleep, and I'm dreaming. It's not just a dream. It's really happening."

"What do you mean, really happening?" she asks.

"Look, this morning I saw my self... Right here... Looking in the refrigerator. At the time, I didn't know it was me cause I was dreaming. Then when I realized that I was dreaming I knew it was me. Then when I woke up I walked in here and I could feel I was being watched. When I turned around, I saw myself sitting right there, in that chair."

"So you saw yourself?"

"Yes in my dream."

"In your dream."

"As soon as I turned around and saw myself. I, the me that was dreaming, disappeared."

"What do you mean disappeared?"

"That's when the me that was dreaming woke up."

"So you saw yourself disappear?"

"Yes. The me that was dreaming disappeared. He was sitting here eating the pie. The same pie that I was eating in my dream.

"Did you try and talk to him?"

"No, I just told you. The instant I saw him he disappeared. I didn't have time to talk to him. It happened so fast."

"Steven, this is crazy talk... Are you OK?"

"You don't believe me!?..."

"Steven, are you hearing yourself?..."

"I don't believe this. You believe in ghosts and evil spirits haunting the house... But not this, this would have to be impossible."

"Honey..."

"Wait, hold on... the other night, after my mom left and we went to bed. Remember, you said you saw me in the den working on the puzzle? You woke me up. And when we went back to bed, I dreamed I was in there, working on the puzzle, and I saw you! You told me don't to stay up all night. Then you left. Then in my dream I went to the kitchen and opened the cupboard, put the kettle in the sink and turn the water on! It was me who turned on the water! But I didn't know I did it, till I dreamed it. Don't you see? We don't have a ghost! It's me doing all this crazy stuff!"

"Steven, the puzzle and the water in the tea kettle happened on entirely different nights, remember. And you got it backwards the puzzler thing happened after the tea kettle thing. Not the other way around."

"Vicky, I don't know how it's happening but its like I'm time traveling in my dreams. And the time travel thing isn't happening in any sensible order. It's like a broken machine doing its own thing. I don't have any control of it. I'm not choosing to time travel to these places, it's just happening."

Vicky thinks for a minute as she takes eggs out of the frying pan with a spatula and puts them on a plate that already has bacon. She hands the plate to Steven and they both take their plates to the table to sit down to eat. Steven notices the writing pad on the table that has the word Raziel on it and picks it up and shows it to Vicky.

Vicky, look at this! I wrote this in my dream. Before I woke up. When I got up it was here on the table.

Vicky looks at the note pad and struggles a little with pronouncing it.

"Razee....Razeel?... What does it mean?"

"I don't know... But maybe it's important... Remember when I had that dream about my grandmother and it turned out she saw it happen, years ago?"

"Yea, and you didn't believe me then, right?"

"Well what if, instead of my grandmother coming to visit me in my dreams, I traveled back in time to visit her?"

"Steven, you said you were 9 years old in that dream."

"I don't know, maybe that's the way it works. After all, if my grandma saw me back then in this body, she wouldn't recognize me. Recognize me..."

Just then Teddy walks into the kitchen and Steven remembers the time he dreamed he was in the silver car being chased by the police through town.

"Teddy! The other night, after the movie, when we were driving home. We saw a car running from the police, remember?"

"Yea..."

"You saw the driver. I know you did. He saw you too, right? Who did he look like to you?"

Steven turns his back to Teddy and points to his chest so only Vicky can see he's doing this.

"Do I have to answer that?"

"Teddy, just answer your dad."

"He looked like dad."

Steven looks at Vicky, eyes open wide nodding his head up and down. Vicky is looking back at him in disbelief. "I was driving that car, and I saw Teddy looking at me from the back seat," he says.

Chapter 41

Just before noon.

On the reception counter at Hillcrest elementary school, is a decorative cup with pens wrapped in green tape and artificial daisies attached to the non-writing end making it all look like a small flower pot next to the sign-in/sign-out sheet on a clipboard for visitors or parents who want to pick up their children early for appointments. The walls surrounding the bulletin board in the office are covered with art deco self portraits, courtesy of the children from the kindergarten classes. Vicky sits at one of two desks that are divided by a path that leads to a couple of other offices behind the reception counter. Filling in for a full time administrator who's on break the desk which is similar to the one next to it has paperwork, a phone, keyboard, monitor, computer on the floor, and a 5 by 7 family portrait next to a and a miniature gold fish bowl half full of Jolly Ranchers which she occasionally gives to students she feels are deserving of the treats. At the moment there isn't a student volunteer there either and classes are in session making it totally silent, which makes her feel this is the perfect time to do a little personal research on the web.

She takes out the small sheet of paper from the pad with the word "Raziel" on it and types it in the Google search engine. Much to her surprise the search engine returns a list of results. The first thing that catches her sight are pictures of artistic renditions of horrific looking demons with what appear to be bat wings extending from their backs.

"Oh my God," she quietly exclaims, wondering, what kind of Satanic mischief is Steven getting mixed up in? Scary thoughts and of horrific images from scenes she remembers seeing in demon possession movies like the Exorcist, race through her mind. And wishing nothing to do with it or allow any part of it to come near her home, she closes her eyes and whispers a short and to the point, prayer, "Lord, please help us."

Reading further on through the lists of search results she learns that Raziel is the name of the angel of mysteries. Still focused on the demon like image on her computer screen, Vicky wonders to herself, angel, huh? Angel for who's side? The Bible says, even Lucifer was once an angel, but he's better known now as the devil. Vicky doesn't hear Darlene, one of the full time administrators, come in quietly from behind.

"Whatcha working on?" She says, breaking the silence in the room and causing Vicky to nearly fall out of her seat after being startled. Vicky breathes a sigh of relief while holding her hand on her chest as she sees it's just Darlene.

Oh! god, Darlene... You scared the life out of me.

Darlene has a good laugh an apologizes for nearly giving Vicky a hear attack. "I'm sorry dear, I didn't mean to scare you like that. I should've probably made a little more noise when I walked in. What's the matter? Did I catch you trying to hack into the Pentagon?"

Vicky laughs with her, saying, "It's ok. Ah...no, I was just checking to see what this word meant. And I got some very creepy results."

Darlene walks over to get a closer look. And immediately she sees the demon like creatures.

"Oooh, that is scary. What made you look it up?"

"Steven had a dream last night and he wrote this."

"Raziel... Did he hear or see it in a movie or something?"

"I don't know, Darlene. He said he didn't know what it meant either. Only that he wrote it while he was still sleeping."

Darlene feels the chills and the small hairs on the back of her neck standing on end. Being a big fan of scary movies, now she feels like she just got cast into the part of generic friend in danger of being next in line to get hacked to pieces by the unstoppable killer hiding just around the corner. "Vicky... this is giving me goose bumps. Now I know why you jumped when I walked in."

"Darlene, you don't even know the half of it."

In a dead silence they both look closely at the image on the computer screen, and the school bell rings nearly causing both of them to scream. Then they laugh it off again.

*

4:30 p.m.

Trying to sell the handgun has proven to be more difficult then Joey originally anticipated. Everyone he knows isn't interested unless he's willing to hand it over to them on credit. But he doesn't trust them, knowing they would probably just take the gun and turnaround and just sell it to someone else for a profit and probably just end up getting burned themselves, and in turn burning him as he waited for payment. On the flip side of this whole gun selling fiasco, the more people Joey tells that he's trying to sell it, the greater the chances are that the cops will catch wind of his illegal gun peddling and probably set up a sting on him.

Right now Joey is sitting out on the plastic patio chair smoking and drinking, and talking on his cell phone with another perspective buyer. "OK, bro. Well, thanks for calling and not leaving me hanging."

"It's not personal dude... Just that $300 is a little steep and..."

"I hear you. It's just that if I go any lower, than that, I'm taking too much of a loss on my end."

"Would you be willing to give me $200 now, take the gun and give me the rest on consignment?"

"Sorry man, no can do."

"OK, well if you change your mind give me a call."

"OK, man, gotta go."

"OK... later, dude."

Another non-taker. Not looking good. Probably best if I just hang low and stop trying to sell the gun for awhile, Joey thinks. Otherwise I could end up in jail with Jeff and Carl. Joey takes a drink, swallows then puffs his cigarette. Tina appears at the open sliding door dressed for work in a low-cut blouse and tight slacks. "Are you going to keep the car while I'm at work?" she asks.

"Yea, why?"

"Debbie want me to come in a little early tonight to learn the new cash register they just got. I need a ride."

"Why is it that you have to go in early? Why doesn't she stay late?"

"She is staying late. But what's the big deal? They're gonna pay me for the extra time."

*

The early evening drive to Lucy's Bar and Grill is only about 10 to 15 minutes from where Tina and Joey live. Joey doesn't even need to use the freeway if he doesn't mind stopping for a few more red light signals along the way, and usually he prefers driving through the business district just to get a feel for what's happening on the main drag. He also has the car stereo blaring a punk rock song that he's pretending to like and is faking like he singing along with so that he doesn't have to speak any nonsense with Tina at the moment.

"How's the gun selling going?" Tina asks.

Joey lowers the volume a little. "What?"

"I said, How's the gun selling going?"

"OK... I gotta friend who knows a guy from out of town who might be interested," Joey says, completely lying about it, knowing how much Tina is against the whole issue of having the gun around in the first place. The less she knows the better. But in the meantime something needs to be said to keep her off his back, he thinks.

"I get out at 2:00 tonight," she says.

"No prob... I'll be there at midnight."

Joey pulls the car into Lucy's parking lot and stops near the front door without parking. Tina gets out shuts the door and Joey drives off before anymore words can be exchanged.

Chapter 42

11:30 p.m.

Parked in a secluded dark corner in one of the eight parking lots that are scattered around the perimeter of Trenton Park, Joey and Christina are finishing up their latest wrestling match of love making. Usually they check into a motel or take their affair to Tina's apartment, but tonight Joey doesn't have the spare money and he got nervous when he saw the neighbor sitting out in her front porch of the apartment next door. That's all he needs, nosey neighbors to go and tell Tina he's having another girl visit while she's out. Putting their clothes back on, Joey notices that the windows are steamed up from the inside, even though he left them open a crack to try and prevent that from happening. He rolls the windows down all the way to give the cool breeze a chance clear up the front and back windshield.

"Joey why don't you make any noise when we're doing it?" Christina asks.

Irritated by the question, Joey says sarcastically, "I learned all my love making techniques from watching silent porn's."

"Come on, Joey. I like it when a man makes noise. It lets me know he's really enjoying himself. You can do that for me."

"What? What do you want? You want me to holler like Tarzan or something? Enough already."

The thought of it makes Tina smile and laugh on the inside as she thinks to herself how funny it would be to hear her lover holler like Tarzan right at the moment of climax. Tarzan movies would never be the same to her again. "That's funny, Joey... Yea! I want to hear a Tarzan yell. Next time we do it, you need to yell like Tarzan."

"Your kidding, right?"

"No really, I want to hear you make a Tarzan yell, right when you finish. You need to promise me that the next time we do it, you're going to give me a Tarzan yell. "

Joey isn't game for what he feels is a stupid childish joke that makes himself the punch line and the only payoff is giving her something to laugh at. As far as he's concerned, he's in it for one thing only, and if there isn't anything for him to get out of it, count him out. And if she isn't in it for the same reason then too bad for her. "Well, don't hold your breath sister," he tells her.

"Joey, have you ever wanted to be a father?" she asks.

Joey suddenly turns looking directly at Christina. Obviously upset, he angrily asks her, "Are you pregnant?!"

Perfect. Just the reaction she was hoping for. He doesn't care about nothing or anyone but himself. Never did, never will. He deserves every little scratch of irritation this stressful position imposes on him. Christina knows now that she's going to enjoy this more than she originally expected.

"Well, I'm a late," she says.

Joey's heart rate skips a beat and kicks into high gear, at the same time his blood pressure rises as his nerves get the best of him causing a slight quiver in his voice to accompany anger, "Aww crap! Christina!," he says, "Don't pull this on me now!! You're joking right!? Tell me right now that this is just a joke!"

"You don't need to get mad Joey," she says, totally in control, and quite pleased with the way this is all playing out so far.

"Well we need to get an abortion... ain't there places that'll do it for free?"

"Forget it Joey. I ain't getting an abortion. I'm Catholic. I don't believe in that."

"You don't have a choice. I'm saying you are. Are you even sure it's mine?"

"I'm not sleeping with anyone else, Joey."

"Then you have to abort it. If you don't, I'll kill you."

"So you're saying that being a father is the worse thing that could possibly happen to you. Even worse than going to jail for murder for the rest of your life?"

"No being a father isn't the worst thing that could happen to me. It's just not part of my master plan."

"Well it isn't gonna happen now. It'll be nine months from now."

"You know what I mean. I don't want to be a

father. Not now, not nine months from now. I think there are places that will do the abortion for you at the governments expense. Kind of like if you were on welfare or something. "

"Joey I'm not having an abortion, no matter who pays for it. And if anything happens to me, you know you would be the first person the police would suspect."

"What do you mean the police?"

"You just threatened to kill me, and your baby. That would make it a double murder. And the only man I've been dating has been you. Everyone knows about us. Except Tina of course."

"Ok, ok... Relax, nobody's getting killed, I just said that cause I was upset. You haven't told anyone else that you're pregnant, have you?"

"Just my friend, Kelly. Why?"

" Who's Kelly?"

"She's a close friend of mine. You never met her. Don't worry, Tina doesn't know her either."

"Good. I don't want any of this to get back to Tina and screw things up for me."

"Don't worry about Tina, Joey. She won't find out about us or the baby."

"Would you quit calling it a baby!"

Christina isn't really pregnant. This is just part of her plan to squeeze Joey for some easy cash. After all, why shouldn't she profit from the hard effort she's been putting into crushing this low life scumbag into the dirt, just before she exposes him for what he is, to Tina.

"OK already. Look, I know of a place that will do an abortion for about $600, and they'll keep the whole thing quiet. Nobody has to know about it. But I need to pay for it all up front. Cash."

"$600 , huh? You can't find any place to do it cheaper?"

"Damn you Joey! That is cheap!"

"Can you pay for half?"

"Joey, I don't even believe in abortion. So if the fact that I'm even willing to do this just to help you out of this mess, isn't good enough, then just forget about the whole thing. I'll just keep my baby and sue you for child support for the rest of your life. And how long do you think you can expect to keep that a secret from Tina?

Joey sits quietly for a moment thinking, about what a mess he's gotten himself into. He does have one more check to pick up from work. But how would he be able to explain the missing $300 to Tina. Maybe I can sell some drugs to make up the difference. Or not. Jeff and Carl getting caught while Joey stays free to roam the streets, makes him like kryptonite in the drug business. The word on the streets is that Joey is the prime suspect that set them up for arrest. Carl himself is probably already making plans on how he's going to get his revenge on Joey. Tina is his only friend right now. And not losing her would be worth far more then the $300 it would cost to keep Christina quiet.

"You're right. Don't worry. Look, I get paid in a couple of days. I'll get you the $600 then. Till then I don't want to hear another word about babies or you being pregnant. Let's get out of here, I gotta go pick up Tina."

Joey starts the car and drives Christine home.

Chapter 43

1:30 a.m.

Sitting at the bar with his new drinking buddy Gary, who was already here when he arrived about half an hour ago, Joey is starting to enjoy the euphoria induced by the intoxicating brew he's been drinking to open the gates of induced reality giving him the temporary escape he's craving more than the fluid he's consuming.

Tina is still bartending, and getting more frustrated at Joey by the minute with the fact that he doesn't seem to understand that his being out spending money like this, after being fired from work less than two days ago is wrong. She knows that without his income, they're not going to be able to afford this kind of extra spending.

In the meantime, Joey is getting drunker by the minute and rambling on about how he was fired unfairly from his job. "...then that a-hole had the nerve to go spy on me when I'm in the crapper... five minutes! Sure I made a phone call, but it was only five minutes! Five minutes! What kind of a-hole fires his fellow employee for being in the toilet for five minutes?!"

Overhearing Joey's spill about being on the phone draws Tina's interest. Joey had previously told her that he was fired for being falsely accused of stealing. Now she's hearing a story about being in the bathroom for five minutes. "You told me someone was stealing from your department and framed you," she says to Joey.

"Oh yeah. That too."

"So which is it? Were you fired for stealing or for an unauthorized bathroom break?"

"What difference does it make? Being fired is being fired."

"The difference is that you lied to me if it wasn't about stealing."

"I didn't lie to you. They fired me for stealing but I was in the bathroom when they decided to nail it on me. I told you it was a set up from the get go."

Gary likes hearing about the drama from Joeys miserable world. It gives him the personal satisfaction of knowing that his own problems aren't so bad after all. "You should sue them," he says.

"Nah... forget them... Who needs that head ache?... Hey, did I ask you if you know anybody who wants to buy a gun?"

Standing right across the bar from Joey, Tina can't believe she just heard Joey bring up the subject of the gun while in his current condition. Her worst fear is that he possibly pull it out from behind his back to show it off to this guy who he just met.

Angrily she tells him, "Joey, don't bring that crap in here."

Although he is drunk right now, Gary is instantly fascinated, as he asks, "You gotta gun, dude?"

"Yea, you want to buy it?"

"You should use it to rob that butt-hole ex-boss of yours! Make him piss his pants! That's what I would do," Gary says.

"You know, that's not a half bad idea," Joey says.

They both laugh... And Joey takes a drink as he ponders the idea.

Chapter 44

3:00 a.m.

Steven is home in bed dreaming.

He dreams he's in the batting cage swinging and hitting pitches and when he sees Raziel, he stops batting. The pitching machine stops as if it knew what Steven's mind set was. Entering a dream has now become similar to waking up from a dream in the sense that now he needs to take into consideration the possibility that the place where he is real. Even dreaming of being at the batting cages doesn't escape his suspicion. Although he never has any recollection of Raziel in the real world, in his dream world he recognizes her immediately along with all the history they have been through together in his past dreams. "Raziel, am I going to die?" he asks her concerned with the dream he had where he saw the thief holding the gun to his head."

"Everyone dies eventually, Steven."

"No. I mean. Am I gonna die soon?"

"Steven, even I don't know your future?"

"Raziel, I saw a man pointing a gun to my head. And I heard the gunshot as I was dream traveled away."

"You saw the future."

"All I have to do is never go to that place again right?... As long as I stay away, I can avoid the confrontation and I should live, right? Tell me I'm right about this."

"You don't have a choice, Steven. You saw yourself there, so it is now your destiny. You will be there. And what you saw happen, will happen. On that exact day. At that exact time. Exactly the way you saw it happen."

Not giving in to the concept of not having any control what so ever, concerning any future event as serious as the end of his life, Steven doesn't intend to go down without a fight.

"Well, I don't plan to just show up and lay my life down without trying to do something about it. I'm not going to be way I saw myself in that dream. I have the advantage of foresight. I have this super power. I can change the outcome."

Raziel knows his foresight won't have any influence on what he's seen in his dream. Knowing where and how the hammer will drop will never stop it from dropping. She knows that what Steven has seen, will happen. And there is nothing she or he can do to stop it from coming to pass. Her composure and attitude now seem to be void of compassion and seem to lack any concern for Steven's demise. "Steven," she calmly tells him, "Everything you do from here on will lead you to that moment. You will change nothing. And whoever told you, you possessed a super power?"

The batting cages and all his surroundings are instantly transformed into the interior of what appears to be a small convenient store. Looking out the window and seeing someone at a gas pumps it becomes evident that he is inside the store of a gas station. Steven has dream traveled back to 1984 and he is inside store of the same gas station where his father was killed. Raziel is standing with him by the magazine rack. Facing the gas pumps Steven immediately recognizes his fathers car parked outside next to the pumps and he sees his father Luke at the rear of his car pumping gas.

"Raziel, what am I doing here? This is just a dream right? Tell me this isn't real. I'm dreaming this right?" he whispers nervously, knowing what is about to happen.

"Look closely, Steven. Don't close your eyes. You once asked me why your father died. From here you will get your answer. You were brought here for no other reason. I'm sure of it."

Steven now smells the odor coffee in the air and he hears a clerk nervously pleading for his life and he looks to his right just in time to see the clerk handing all the money in a bag to the robber, then the robber punches the clerk in the face knocking him to the ground and before Steven thinks do anything, the thief rushes out the front door.

Steven feels his body grow weak, numb and powerless as he stands by helplessly watching. Just outside right in front of him the thief trips and falls to the ground as a cat darts away and the gun in the thief's hand fires. Steven sees his father clutch his chest and fall to the ground. Completely overwhelmed by having to relive this moment and the horror of knowing now that he was right here in the same place and didn't do anything to stop it from happening, Steven covers his face in his hands crying silently, as Raziel starts to glow from the overflowing sorrow Steven is experiencing. Then he senses a chill from a drop in temperature as his environment changes and the tears on his face are gone as he dream travels into the future.

He's still in a convenient store, but it's not the same store. Nor is he in the past anymore. Raziel is not with him now and he sees that the chill he felt came from the beverage cooler he's standing by further into the back of the store. He hears a commotion taking place at the register, which draws his attention to the fact that he is no longer in the past and has returned to a familiar place that he has dreamed of before. He turns around and slowly walks towards the checkout counter, where he sees a man wearing a ski mask and pointing a gun at the clerk. The clerk standing behind the register counter with his hands held up is almost in tears frightened for his life. The man in the ski mask who is getting angrier by the minute, shouts at him relentlessly, "...I mean it I'll shoot you in the head sucker!! Don't give me any crap!... Don't move!!"

Steven doesn't remember any of this from a dream or any real life experience he's had in the past. But he does recognize the clerk behind the counter. He's the same clerk from a flash dream he had before. But this wasn't in that dream. "Could this be a different dream of a different time," he wonders.

"OK, OK, ...don't sh... , please don't shoot me," the clerk pleads.

"Shut up!!...Move away from the register!... Go! Get out of there!... Keep your hands up!"

The clerk moves away from the register. And the masked thief hurries around to the other side and tries to open it, keeping the gun aimed at the clerk.

He pushes buttons and gets more upset that the drawer doesn't open. After a few failed attempts he looks at the clerk and puts two hands on the gun he has aimed at him. Then he notices Steven slowly walking from about 10 feet away along the refrigerated soft drinks aisle.

"What the?!? Where'd you come from?!!" he shouts at Steven and directs the aim of his gun at him.

Steven raises his hands in the air displaying no weapons or any threat to the thief, as he calmly says, "I'm just a customer here... Just like you."

"Oh, you're a comedian! I bet you think your real funny? Don't move!!"

The gunman moves right next to the clerk and puts the gun right up against the back of his head, and says, "You think you're funny, huh? You move. He gets a bullet in the head!"

Steven knows he's just dreaming, but he also senses this is real, a bullet flying to the head of the clerk, from point blank range is something he won't be able to stop. If the gunman pulls the trigger, there would be nothing he could do to save the clerks life. His only option is to negotiate.

"No. You don't need to do that... Nobody's gonna try and stop you."

"Shut up! Just shut up, you!"

Standing behind the clerk, the gunman holds him by his shirt with one hand and the gun pressed to his head with the other.

"Listen a-hole, if you want to live you better open the cash register."

"Just calm down and relax, dude," Steven says to the clerk.

"I said shut up, you!!"

"Look if you want the register open, you need to make this man relax and not be in fear of his life."

"What? What are you talking about?"

"He can't open the register if his hands are shaking so much because he's in fear for his life. Just talk normal to him and he'll do what you ask. Don't worry we won't try and stop you. The important thing is nobody gets hurt."

"Ok, then, You!"

"Calmly."

"Listen you, start moving back to the register. I want you to open it. Then just back off. Is that better?"

Steven doesn't move as he watches with his hands up, and the clerk moves towards the register and opens it, then the gunman pushes him back to the other end then grabs the money out of the drawer and stuffs in in his pockets. All this happening while he keeps the gun pointing at the clerk. Then he pulls out the money tray and throws it on the floor and grabs what ever cash he can quickly grab hold of. Feeling quite confident now, as if his task is complete and he's performed a job well done, the thief raises his arm and gives a left hand salute. "Nice doing business with you," he says, maneuvers around the counter, and hurries to the front door. Just before he gets to the door he reaches for the newspaper rack, he pulls it, causing the papers to fall out scattering all over the floor in front of the doorway. Then once out the door he pulls off his ski mask and goes to his left.

Steven feels good from the fact that the clerk wasn't killed. He feels that the person he was sent here to rescue has been saved and now he can dream travel away having accomplished his required deed.

Then as he and the clerk both start lowering there arms, Steven remembers this store and this dream more clearly. It's not a new dream of a different time or place, but instead a bigger piece of the puzzle from the segment of the flash dreams he's had before. There's a loud startling shot from outside. The clerk ducks down and Steven's reacts by looking to his left and running towards the front door. He already knows what he's going to see outside as he makes for the exit. Running to the door he looks down and notices newspapers scattered on the floor. This time he sees the front page headline clearly, "DISASTER IN THE GULF," it reads, and sees there's a picture of a burning offshore oil rig below it. He takes care so as not to slip on the scattered papers as he rushes to the door. Then pushing the door open, he goes through and stops and he sees the Circle K sign out at the corner near the street. He turns immediately to his left and about 15 feet away, one knee on the ground, holding his stomach, he sees the man that looks very much like himself. Standing between he and the man is the thief who just left the store, holding the gun to his head. Steven has already seen the outcome of this event. He knows that the man down on one knee is himself. And he doesn't intend to allow what he saw happen once before happen again. Steven hears the gunman say, "I'm sorry dude, but you know what I look like."

Steven knows what is coming next but he only needs to get close enough to the gunman to either knock him down or deflect his aim, anything to change the outcome could be the key. He knows what Raziel said about not being able to change what he already seen happen. But just maybe. With his power of super speed maybe he could change what it is he needs to, just enough to give his other self a chance at life. He just needs to get close enough to touch him. He launches himself forward with all his might concentrating his inner effort at making himself move towards the shooter with the same super fast ability he used back when he confronted the two thugs harassing the hot dog vender. As fast as he can he moves to try and stop him but instead he merely manages to take one leaping step as the Steven on the ground looks up at him and makes eye contact. The gunman squeezes the trigger point blank directly at Stevens head, and everything disappears as Steven wakes up, hearing the gunshot in the fading oblivion.

Chapter 45

Wednesday
5:45 a.m.

Home in bed, Steven wakes up in a sudden jolt startled from the shooting and at the same time he unintentionally wakes up Vicky who was sleeping comfortably next to him. He sits up deeply concerned that he's going to be killed and there could have been something he should have done differently, as Vicky asks him, "Steven?... Are you OK?"

Steven quickly tries to composes himself. But he's still shaking with fear, and trying not to show it.

"Yea, I'm fine... just a nightmare," Steven says, trying not to let Vicky see how serious he's concerned with what he just dreamed of.

"Was it about that demon?" she asks, not letting him off the hook.

"Demon? What are you talking about?" Steven asks , and is now curious about what Vicky is implying.

"Raziel."

"Raziel?"

"I didn't tell you yesterday but I Google searched that word at work yesterday and it said he's an angel of mystery or something... but you won't believe the pictures. If you ask me he looks more like a demon."

*

Sitting at the Kitchen table with the laptop before her Vicky types the word Raziel on the Google search engine and the list of results pop up. Standing behind and leaning in over her shoulder to see what it is, Vicky was talking about, Steven peers into the screen and the artistic renderings of the angel Raziel catches his eye.

"Does any of this remind you of your dream?" Vicky asks.

Steven doesn't recall ever dreaming of any angels, or demons for that matter. If he had dreamed of anything even close to that, he's pretty sure he would've remembered it. "No. I didn't dream anything like that... Angle of mystery, huh? Not even close," he says.

"So then tell me. What was your nightmare about?" she asks.

Remembering seeing himself on his knees with the gun pointing at his head, Steven decides it better not to worry Vicky and plays down what he dreamt about. "It was just a dream about a store robbery, then a guy got shot...no big deal."

"Steven, I'm going to schedule a Dr.'s appointment for you. I don't think it's healthy. You sleep too deeply. It seriously scares the life out of me. Not to mention it looks like it's the life is out of you when you're deep asleep."

"Vicky..."

"I'm not taking no for an answer. Maybe you could be suffering from sleep apnea or something. I've heard of that before. You could really stop breathing in your sleep and end up dying. You're going to see a doctor about it. I'll even take you there myself if I have to. Now, I gotta get ready for work. Can you do me a favor and wake up the boys for school?"

"All right. Anything to keep the peace in this home."

Closing the laptop shut, Vicky gets up from her seat and heads for her morning shower.

Steven gets up and goes to the boy's room, knocks and opens the door. Both Erick and Teddy are sleeping in their bunk beds, and they reluctantly start waking up.

"Guys... wake up... Time to get ready for school... Come on, get up."

Steven then goes back through the living room still wondering what he should have done differently in his dream. He walks to the front door to get the morning newspaper. "If only I could have got my hands on the thug, I could have taken him apart. But the Steven on the ground looking at me caused me to wake up and disappear from the dream. Maybe I should have tackled and disarmed him before he got out the door. Before he made a mess spilling the newspapers all over the floor. He did it on purpose. He probably made the mess thinking it would stop me from following him out the door." Still thinking about the newspapers he clearly sees the headline in his mind, DISASTER IN THE GULF, right above the photo of a burning offshore oil rig, out in the ocean. He comes to the conclusion that what he needs to do is dream the same dream again and the next time he's going to do everything he has to do to keep the thug from getting out the front door. That's it, problem solved. Tonight when I go to sleep I can set everything straight.

Opening the front door, Steven feels confident his problems are back in his court. Once again he's the master of his fate, in total control, having solved his dilemma with a creative solution. What am I even concerning myself over, he thinks again, it was all just a dream. Reaching down and picking up the morning paper, he pulls off the rubber band and opens up the paper to the front page. Slowly his jaw falls open and a chill runs up his spine as his dream world and reality collide again right before his eyes. There in his hands, on the front page of today's paper, in bold capital letters. DISASTER IN THE GULF. And right below it, the photo of an offshore oil rig, on fire, out in the ocean water.

Chapter 46

9:30 a.m.

At first Steven was hesitant to leave the house for his morning run. The headline on the front page was identical to the one he dreamed of. He didn't tell Vicky or the boys anything about the newspaper headline or about the dream of him being shot. Worrying them wouldn't be of any help. The boy's would just think their dad is going crazy. And Vicky would probably have him go see a doctor this morning. Probably a psychiatrist. No, better not to even mention anything about the dream or the newspaper headline. There would be now way to convince anyone that he were even telling the truth. All he has to do is not go anywhere near a Circle K convenience store.

Running through the neighborhood along his usual route, his mind flashes back to his dream, where he's standing with his hands up and looking at the clerk.

Still jogging.

He sees himself standing out in front of the convenient store.

Jogging.

Looking at himself down on one knee with the gun pointed to his head.

Jogging, he slows down to a walk, breathing heavily then stops and rests in place with his hands on his knees.

"All I gotta do is stay home today," he says.

*

Joey walks through the automatic front doors at Wal-Mart, a little nervous and slightly hung-over but ready to enforce his revenge. He notices one of the undercover security guards standing at one of the checkout lines chatting with one of the cashier clerks. Sizing up the guard, he can tell from where he is that the guard stands at least 5 inches taller than himself and probably outweighs him by 50 pounds.

Continuing on he heads straight for the break room, and right into the managers office, where he finds Mikey sitting behind his desk studying a sales report. Mikey looks up from the report and sees Joey.

"Hey, Joey," he says, "If your here for your check, your too late. The mails already been sent out."

Joey pulls the gun out from behind his back and puts it to Mikey's head. Mikey raises his hands nervously in submission, begging for mercy, "Please don't shoot me, Joey. Please don't . What do you want? Anything... You want your job back? Anything, just name it."

"Shut up, Mikey, where's the money?"

Mikey points to a canvas bag on the floor and Joey goes to the bag, opens it to look inside and sees about ten stack of $100 bills wrapped in stacks of 100's. Then the big security guard that Joey had seen earlier comes in from the break room and Joey pistol whips him with the gun over the head knocking him out cold. Mikey stands up yelling at Joey, "What did you do?!!"

"Shut up!!!" Joey says, and looks and laughs at Mikey seeing that the front of his trousers are wet.

"Who's the boss now!"

Joey runs out of the office, through the break room and out through the main store. The other workers and shoppers see him with the gun and stop in their tracks backing away in fear.

When Joey reaches the front exits he hollers, "Woo-hoo!!!, as he fires his gun in the air. Some of the female employees scream in fear, and Joey goes out the front door.

Right outside the front door the security guard that Joey pistol whipped in the break room punches Joey smack in the jaw spinning him around and dropping him to the ground. Then he cuffs Joey's wrist behind his back.

"You're going to be in prison for a long time, boy," the security guard says.

"Joey?" Mikey says.

Joey stands a little dazed in Mikey's office.

"Joey? Hello... I said your check was mailed out already." Mikey says again.

Snapping back to reality, Joey stands silently staring right past Mikey trying to replay the events he just imagined in his mind. Trying to work in a more favorable ending for himself. The big security guard walks in and breaks Joeys concentration and Joey looks at him nervously. "Are you OK, bro?" he says.

"Joey... I said your check was mailed," Mikey says again, as the security guard takes a seat and thumbs through a magazine.

Joey looks at the security guard, then back at Mikey and decides on the spot to abort the mission. This isn't the right time. No, I need to plan this better.

"Joey!" Mikey says, getting impatient, and beginning to get suspicious.

"What?" Joey says as if he was being interrupted.

"Are you OK? What do you want?"

"What?"

"What are you doing here?"

Looking back at Mikey, Joey doesn't answer. Instead he just leaves the office quickly without saying anything.

Mikey doesn't trust Joey, and he waits till Joey is out of earshot before he tells the security guard, "Stay with him. Keep a close eye on him. I don't trust that guy." The guard nods in acknowledgment and gets up from his seat and leaves the office to follow Joey and make sure he causes no problems.

Leaving the store, Joey heads to the car feeling as if he is a failure. I suck, he thinks to himself. But I would've gotten myself arrested if I tried to rob this place. I need to think it out more. Plan better. I'm not a coward. I know can do this. I just need a practice target.

*

11:00 a.m.

Sitting at the kitchen table, Steven stares at the

screen of the lap top. Monster dot com displays a list of possible job opportunities. One in particular holds his attention at the moment. It's a local construction company right here in his home town. Probably less than a 10 minute drive from his front door. It would be a dream come true to work for a company so close to home. All his life he's never had a commute less than 30 minutes to work.

He looks down at the newspaper front page sitting on the table and stares at the dreaded headline. "All I have to do is stay home today," he thinks to himself. But it was just a dream. It isn't real. He closes his eyes and thinks back to his dream.

Standing in the store facing the clerk, they both have their hands raised. He can see that the clerk is shaken from the events that led up to this moment. Then the clerk flinches and ducks as he hears the gunshot from outside, and Steven makes for the front double glass doors, and sees the papers on the floor. The front page, DISASTER IN THE GULF, and the photo of the burning offshore oil rig. Focusing now as much to detail as possible, he counts the water jets shooting from the fireboats in the water around the rig. Three from the center to the right. And a small group of what could be three from the left side. Another fire fighter boat, red and white, on the way in the foreground of the sea.

Opening his eyes, Steven looks again at the photo on the front page. In every way, down to the last detail, the picture is exactly the same as the one he dreamed of.

But it was just a dream, he reminds himself. And if not, I still have the advantage of foresight. All I have to do is not go to a Circle K convenient store, today. I go apply for the job, secure the interview. Get the job, then come straight home. Everything will be just fine. It was just a dream.

He goes to his bed room and quickly puts on a white dress shirt and a pair of dress pants. Then he goes to the bathroom to comb his hair. While washing his face he realizes that he still hasn't shaved so he starts shaving. While shaving he nicks himself on the neck and a couple of drops of blood stain the collar of his shirt, so he takes it off and tries to scrub it out with cold water but it only dilutes the stain and spreads further into the collar as a big pink spot, so he sprays it with stain remover, tosses into the laundry and goes to the closet to get a replacement. Completely forgetting what he was wearing when he saw himself get killed in his dream he takes out the same exact light blue dress shirt.

Chapter 47

12:57 p.m.

In the parking lot, sitting in his car, Steven waits for 1:00 to tick on his clock. He doesn't want to show up to close to the 12:00 hour, only to be told everyone's out to lunch. The combination of the fresh air and being out here, looking for a job has put his mind at ease now. The dream he had this morning is now filed away and sitting in storage in a cabinet in the basement of his memory labeled ridiculous things to talk about later. His focus now is to impress the owner or the superintendent of this company, enough to believe hiring him would be of great benefit to their business and not hiring him would be the biggest mistake of their careers. 12:59, close enough. Steven gets out of the car and goes inside the building.

*

Not far from where Steven is, Joey is walking

from his car and toward a Circle K convenient store that he scoped. It's the perfect practice target. Staked out across the street in his car, Joey watched the store for about half an hour and convinced himself that this was the perfect place to practice for the big hit. Even if he doesn't get a lot of cash from this job, he will get experience that may come in useful on his next job. He parked the car down the street about half a block away, near an elementary school, so nobody from the store will be able to trace the plates back to him, just in case an employee followed him out to the parking lot, or security camera's were filming outside. It wouldn't be likely that anyone would follow him away from the parking lot. And if they tried, he'd shoot them. Now he walks calmly with the hand gun loaded, safety off, tucked in his lower back of his pants, and a ski mask in his pocket. It's show time.

*

Steven walks out of the building, disappointed by the fact that the company had already filled the job opening. They took a copy of his resume and told him they would keep him in mind, should things pick up, but didn't have any good news for him concerning the near future. Even though he's only just got laid off, he walks to his car, slightly depressed by the thought that so many people are out of work and nobody seems to be hiring. "I know I just got laid off but how long this dry spell will last?"

When he reaches the door to his car, he sees something that makes his jaw drop. Something he didn't notice when he parked in this spot earlier. Less than half a block from where he parked his car he sees the corner street sign of a Circle K convenience store.

He remembers his dream and the conversation he had with himself concerning his fate. The future is yours to choose. But once you see it, it has become a part of your past. Like a prophecy, and there's nothing you can do to change it. Every path you take, and every decision you make, will inevitably lead you to the event unfolding exactly as you saw it happen. As if he were in a hypnotic trans, no longer in control of his own actions he walks away from his car and towards the convenient store. Walking calmly without fear, yet with no purpose or plan, he's moving the way he did when he dreamed he was going into the auto body shop. On auto pilot. Only this time he knows where he's going and he knows the fate that awaits him.

Crossing the road, he doesn't even notice the police car with two cops sitting in it, parked on the street with the motor running, and facing the same direction he's walking.

Chapter 48

Steven walks towards the convenient store in a trance still hearing his own voice, convincing himself that he needs to be here for his fate. Like an animal being led to slaughter, he continues without reason or choice. With no option of changing what he knows is meant to be. He doesn't understand why he's doing this, only that he has to. He loves his wife and two sons, and understands that his death would be devastating to them. But he feels he has no choice now. This event is beyond his right or ability to choose. He has no other option here. Only a path which he knows he will follow, because it already happened. He hears his own voice telling him, "You will be there, Steven. What you saw will happen. On that exact day. At that exact time. Exactly the way you saw it happen."

Steven continues walking, and hearing his own voice.

"You have no choice."
"You have no choice."
"You have no choice."
The loud crack of gunfire snaps him out of his trans as he looks out at the store from the sidewalk, stunned by what he sees.

*

The two cops sitting in the parked patrol car hear and recognize the sound of the gunshot and immediately respond. The driver shifts the car into gear and peels out, as his partner picks up the radio mike and reports the possible shots fired, and unit responding.

*

Stunned by what he's looking at, Steven stands watching from the sidewalk out in front and near the left end of the parking lot. At the right front corner of the store he sees himself down on one knee and holding his stomach, and the shooter, walking towards him, pointing the gun. Then to his surprise he sees himself again, come out the front door, briefly looking out at the Circle K sign at the corner, then turn left and stop in his tracks, for a moment. At this point there are now three Stevens here at this same moment in time. The Steven at the front door lunges at the gunman as the Steven on the ground looks up, and simultaneously the two Stevens disappear as Joey fires the weapon just missing the Steven down on one knee. Then Joey looks around confused and angry. He sees Steven standing out in the sidewalk by the driveway, then he sees the police car driving up lights flashing and he takes off running in the other direction, across the small parking lot and down the street. The police car spots Joey, turns on the siren and chases him up the road. Then an innocent bystander, woman nervously pokes her head out from behind the corner of the store, as if to see if the danger has cleared.

*

Fleeing from police and the scene of the robbery, Joey decides not to try and get to his car, but instead, make his escape on foot through the elementary school, then possibly through the schoolyard and over a fence and out into the adjoining neighborhood streets. Running as fast as he can, he reaches the front entrance of the Hillcrest Elementary School gated entrance where he knows the patrol car won't fit through. He cuts through the entrance. The patrol car stops in the parking lot just out in front of the school, and both cops jump out and take off after him as fast as they can run.

*

Mr. Barns, the 4th grade teacher who doesn't appear a day over 30 is out at the edge of the playground sitting on a small folding chair reading a novel, while his students are out on the playground running around playing with other classes during recess. The school hires part-time playground supervision and he doesn't need to be out here but unlike most of the other teachers who take their breaks in the staff lounge, he prefers to be out here for his afternoon break. This is the last recess of the day and being out here at this exact spot in the shade has become an important part of his daily routine.

*

As Joey comes running down the exterior corridor with the gun in hand and he sees the kids on the playground out past the end of the corridor. If necessary he feels he'll be able grab and hold one of the kids, and get the cops to back off their pursuit long enough give him a better head start. The school bell rings and a teacher opens her classroom door, and bumps Joey, causing him to squeeze the trigger, firing the gun. Pandemonium breaks out in the playground as kids scream and run in different directions. It isn't immediately evident if anyone has been struck by the bullet till Mr. Barns at the other end of the corridor, drops to the ground off his chair right in front of Teddy, Steven's son, who's holding a kick ball and is looking at Mr. Barns in shock. Mr. Barns looks up at Teddy and says, "Teddy, get down on the ground."

Teddy throws the ball and drops to the ground taking cover. Right next to Mr. Barns. "Does it hurt?," he asks.

"I've never been shot before. Yeah, I guess I would say yes, it hurts. It hurts a lot. Just stay down."

Teddy doesn't move and is starting to feel the effects of a little shock from realizing that he's just seen his teacher get shot. Other kids are screaming in horror as they run away out into the playground where they gather with the playground supervisor who's on her radio talking with the office trying to find out what's going on.

With the sound of police sirens blaring in the distance, the two cops tackle Joey to the ground and he drops the gun no longer trying to resist arrest and is a little worried now that he may have just shot a child. Held face down with his hands cuffed behind his back, Joey looks around and sees the school teacher and a student down on the ground, out in the playground at the other end of the corridor.

The school principle and a couple of janitors come from around the side of the building and run out to the injured teacher and holler for someone to call for an ambulance. Vicky and Darlene come out to see all what the commotion is about. Teddy stands up uninjured and sees his mom running to him with tears in her eyes past the police. One who's guarding Joey on the ground cuffed and still laying face down. The other cop is on his radio calling for an ambulance as more police sirens can be heard arriving from a distance.

Chapter 49

About 7:00 p.m.

School employees, family members, some students and parents are in the hospital emergency waiting room, some sitting and others pacing nervously . Steven and Vicky sit and watch as a doctor wearing scrubs comes out and speaks to two women and an elderly man. Judging by their reaction it appears the doctor has given them good news. Then the doctor walks away and back through the double doors, followed by the younger of the two women. Vicky and the school principal get up at the same time and go speak with the older lady and the man who appears to be her husband, wanting to find out what the doctor just said.

Steven sits waiting with Erick and Teddy who have been complaining how tired they are and wondering when they can going home.

"Hey look!" Teddy says, pointing to the TV monitor mounted on the wall and playing in very low volume. "That's our school."

On the TV is an image of the front entrance of the school from across the street. About five police cars and an ambulance can be seen parked out in front then the camera pans over to Tammy Marshal looking very professional in her job holding a mike and giving the details of the shooting.

Vicky returns with the elderly lady to speak with Steven. Steven stands and Vicky introduces her, "Steven, someone wants to meet you. This is Mrs. Barns, Kevin's mother.

"Kevin?" Steven asks Vicky.

"Yes Kevin Barns, Teddy's school teacher, he's the teacher that got shot." Vicky whispers to Steven.

"Call me Margie" she says.

"Oh yes, of course. Margie, how is Kevin?"

"The doctor says, he's going to be laid up in bed for a couple of weeks, but other than that he's going to be fine. Miraculously the bullet didn't hit any major organs. One more centimeter to the left or right could have been fatal. They say it's a miracle."

"Oh, thank god," Steven says.

"Your your name is Steven Farrow, isn't it?"

"Yes ma'am."

"Please, call me Margie."

"OK, Margie, call me Steven."

"Steven, was your father, Luke Farrow?"

"Yes. How did you?"

"Steven, your father, Luke, and my son, Kevin, crossed paths along time ago."

"They knew each other?"

"No, I can't say they did."

"I don't understand."

"This is really hard to say.... I'm not sure how to word this so please forgive me. A long time ago, when your father was killed, Kevin and I were there."

"What?... What do you mean, you were there?"

"Kevin was still just a baby, he was about 11 months at the time. I was driving, and Kevin was strapped in his car seat in the back in his car seat. We pulled up to the gas pumps. I parked my car and was looking through my purse when I heard a very loud gunshot. I turned to look where it came from and I saw your father in the next lane, fall to the ground."

"Why are you telling me this?"

"Steven, I believe your father saved my sons life that night."

Steven is stunned.

"What? How? I don't understand?"

"If the bullet hadn't been stopped by your father, I'm pretty sure it would've hit my little Kevin."

"But how?"

"Steven, I was there, and I saw your father fall to the ground after being shot. I got out of my car and ran around to take Kevin out of his car seat and that's when I knew in my heart, that if your father hadn't been there in that very spot, the bullet would have traveled from where that robber fell directly to where little Kevin was sitting in the back of our car."

Steven thinks back to that night.

*

He's 8 year old and sitting in the front seat with his comic book, looking out the window. From his perspective he sees the car driven by the woman pulling up to the pumps in the next lane. Then he sees the man run out the front door, trip, fall and gun fire. Then looking into the store he sees the strange man with his hands over his face and the ghost woman. Both are inside the store behind the glass.

*

Then Steven he snaps out of that memory, realizing he didn't see his father get shot that night. Not when he was 8 years old. Then he remembers the dream travel he had last night.

*

He's in the store standing by the magazine rack and he recognizes his fathers car. Then he sees his father, pumping gas at the rear of the car Knowing what is about to happen, he thinks to himself, What am I doing here? Then he hears himself saying, "Look closely, Steven. Don't close your eyes. You once asked why your father died. You were brought here for a reason, I'm sure of it." Then he hears a clerk nervously pleading for his life and he looks to his right just in time to see the clerk handing all the money in a bag to the robber. The thief hit's the clerk. And before he can get involved, he sees the thief rush out the front door.

Just outside almost right in front of Steven, the thief trips and falls to the ground as a cat darts away and the gun in the thief's hand fires. Steven sees his father clutch his chest and fall to the ground. As his father falls clutching his chest the car behind him comes into view. Right in the line of fire is 11 month old baby Kevin Barns, in his car seat sucking on a baby bottle. Steven covers his face and doesn't see what follows but his imagination allows him to see the much younger looking Margie Barns, who comes running from the driver side of her car and opens the back door, un-straps her baby, and takes him into her arms.

*

"Steven your father saved Kevin's life a long time ago, that night," Margie tells him, "You were there. And it broke my heart to see you lose your father. For so many years I've wanted to tell you about this but I never knew how to. Now the police tell me your son Teddy could have been killed if Kevin wasn't out there sitting in his spot when that gun was fired today."

"So if my dad hadn't died, Kevin would have. And if Kevin had died back then, Teddy would've died today," Steven says quietly.

Having lived for so long with the unanswered question. He never knew his dad had been in the path of bullet traveling towards a baby. The very baby who would grow up to save his own sons life today. And had he known back then it would be very likely that he wouldn't have understood enough for it to have made much difference to him. The fact that his father had died was a tragedy for which there were no plausible explanation. After what happened today, he realizes that his dad, Luke, didn't just save baby Kevin's life 26 years ago, he also inadvertently saved his own grandsons life today. Steven hugs Margie.

"Thank you for telling me this," he tells her, with tears welling in his eyes. "Your son Kevin is my hero."

Margie hugs Steven, as she remembers back to that night she held her baby in her arms, while Steven not much more than a baby himself wept for his dying father right before her. She begins weeping too as she tells him, "All these years, you and your father have been mine."

Just then Tammy Marshal walks in and is heading towards Margie. "Mrs. Barns," she calls out ahead of her arrival.

"Hi Tammy, please call me Margie. Oh Tammy, this is Steven Farrow and his wife Victoria."

"Hello Tammy, Pleasure to meet you," Steven say, as he reaches out to shake her hand.

"We've met before," Tammy says looking a little quizzical.

"We have?," Steven wonders, thinking back to the time when he dream traveled back when he stole the cops BMW.

"Yes, I know you from somewhere. I never forget a face. It goes with the job. Just give me a second to think about it."

"I promised Tammy the exclusive interview with us when Kevin is feeling better," Margie says.

"And I don't know how to thank you enough. This is going give our hometown station notoriety we've been waiting for, for years. How is Kevin doing?"

"He's doing well, the Dr. says...

Steven starts to leave with Vicky and the boys. As he gets to the door he's stopped from behind by a hand on his shoulder.

"Mr. Farrow!," Tammy says.

Steven turns a little startled.

"Sorry to startle you like that. The convenient store."

"What?"

"I saw you out front at the convenient store where the robbery took place today... We didn't actually meet but that's where I seen you before. I knew I'd seen you somewhere."

Chapter 50

About a month has past and Steven's dream traveling seem to have come to an end. The home front is peaceful once more. There are no more haunting episodes that occurring through the day or in the middle of the night. Nothing is out of place, nor have any strange encounters returned to disrupt the normal flow of the daily routine. Everything seems back to normal.

There was however one night last weekend, when Steven and Vicky were out late, one evening for a romantic getaway having walk on a beach pier. A fisherman who Steven never met before, was at the corner of the pier looking over the edge down into the water shaking his head and muttering something to himself, then he turned and looked strangely at Steven and told him, "Man... I really thought you just jumped from here a minute ago."

"I get that a lot," Steven says, jokingly.

Steven still hasn't found any work, but he, Vicky and the boys have adjusted their lives to the cut in their income. No more going out to the movies. No big birthday parties. No eating out. Steven even skips a meal now and then, which has helped keep him from gaining excessive weight. The important thing is we're still together, Steven reminds himself when he's feeling down.

It's late at night and Steven is now at home in bed next to Vicky reading a novel and he feels himself getting tired so he sets the book on his nightstand and falls asleep and slips into a dream.

*

He's at the batting cages, standing by home plate with a wood bat in hand and though it's been about a month since he was last here it feels to him like it was just a couple of days ago. Raziel is about 10 feet away at the other side of home plate by the screen that divides the batting boxes.

"They think you look like a demon," he tells her.

"They... have no idea who I am."

" Raziel, I saw it. On the computer. There are pictures of what look like demons, but it says they're angels and they have your name identifying them."

"Are you the only human with the name Steven? You know those pictures you saw on the internet are not me, and on top of that, any human who has ever met me doesn't remember me in your world. You already proved that wasn't possible when you wrote my name down on the pad and couldn't understand what it meant. Even after Vicky looked it up on the web."

Steven pauses, looks at the batting machines. Then he looks back at Raziel.

"You were right about my father."

Raziel smiles.

"I understand now," Steven says, "I wouldn't have understood before Teddy almost got killed. But the truth was revealed just when I needed it. Just one thing... Why couldn't you tell me that I wasn't going to get killed, when I told you that I saw myself get shot?.. It could have saved me a lot of worry, you know."

"Like I said, I don't know your future. I didn't know you weren't going to get killed. You told me you saw yourself get shot, and what I told you, was that what you saw happen would come to pass. And it did."

Again, Steven looks back out at the batting machine, thinking about how everything happened at the Circle K store. Raziel was right. Everything happed just the way it did in his dream.

Steven positions himself to hit a pitch. And the batting machine starts up and delivers a pitch that appears to be traveling 200 miles per hour. Steven swings and makes perfect contact, and hears a familiar cheer of his father just outside of the batting cage, " Yes! That's it! Good hit! That's the way to go! Do it again Stevie!"

Raziel smiles and Steven dream travels.

*

Now finding himself out in the parking lot of the Circle K store, Steven knew one day, he would have a dream that would return him here to this precise time and place. He didn't know when it would happen, only that the check was in the mail and he needed to be ready to cash in. From his current placement in the parking lot he is unable to see inside the store to know what is happening. He knows his purpose here isn't just to take a bullet and delay the thief from fleeing the scene of the crime. He's here to prevent harm from coming to someone. Then he sees a woman getting out of her car and preparing to go into the store going in the store. If he doesn't stop her, she's on a head on collision course with the with a man who Steven already knows will shoot anyone who gets in his path. He quickly goes to her car and opens the gas door and unscrews the gas cap. The he calls out to her, "Excuse me, ma'am!"

The woman turns around and Steven that it's Tammy Marshal. At first she ignores him and turns away, probably thinking he's going to ask her for money. But Steven stops her when he tells her, "You're gonna lose your gas cap."

"What?" she asks a little confused as she turns around.

" I'm sorry to bother you, but your gas cap is hanging by a thread from your car," Steven says, as he points back to her car.

Looking back at her car, she now sees that the gas cap is hanging out from the fuel door on the plastic retainer strap that prevents it from falling off.

"Thank you," she says, and walks back to her car.

Steven starts for the corner of the store.

Out in front, Joey shoves the front door open and pulls off the ski mask, then starts to jog toward the corner. A surprised look appears on his face as he sees Steven come around the corner from the other side.

"What the? How did you get out here?" he says and he aims the gun and fires. The bullet hits Steven directly in the stomach and he feels it like it were a stick being jabbed into him. Looking at Joey, Steven drops down on one knee. Then looks downward at his hands seeing them all bloody from the wound to his stomach. Joey moves in close to Steven and presses the gun against his forehead.

"Sorry dude, he says, You saw what I look like."

Steven knows exactly what he needs to do now. He's seen it already when he dreamed it in the past, and he's seen it while awake from the other end of the parking lot out on the sidewalk. The sidewalk? Yes..., there he is, from the corner of his eye he sees his own past. The other Steven. The one who isn't dreaming. Poor guy, thinks he's gonna die, walking faithfully to his predestined death sentence. So he believes this is his swan song. Kind of funny looking back at what was going through your mind. But he's not out of the woods just yet. What happens when this thug pulls the trigger with the gun pointing right at his forehead? Does he die deep in his sleep? Does he wake up? There's no choice but to let play out what he knows has already happened. Steven raises his head and sees his other self lunging forward from behind the gunman and makes eye contact with the other Steven who is lunging at him, and his surroundings instantly change as he dream travels away to the hollow sound of the glock 19 firing in the distance.

Chapter 51

October 26, 2014
7:56 p.m.

Standing in front of a picture window lined with lace curtains Vicky looks through it and into the night outside as she waves bye to a car that drives through a round-about circular driveway and into a stretch that leads out to the main road. The house she's in is obviously beyond the means of anyplace Steven could ever afford to live in with the income from his construction job, even if he pulled double overtime everyday. The furniture and wall hangings are all new, expensive yet modest and in good taste. She walks on beautiful custom flooring and through a spacious entry foyer and down a wide hall past a portrait of herself and the boys relaxing on patio furniture out in a beautifully decorated garden, in the background a manmade waterfall cascading through rocks and into a swimming pool.

A large door opens, and lights on sofa end tables

and over head turn on as Vicky walks in and sits in a large comfortable sofa chair. Motion detectors. Sitting quietly, she looks across the room into mid air a few feet in front of her without any expression that would convey what she's thinking of. The clock on the wall behind her strikes 8:02.

Then he appears. From out of thin air, not a sound of any kind to announce his presence nor a whisper of a hint of any change in atmospheric pressure to account for his sudden manifestation. Vicky gasps from a combination of surprised and fear, then her expression changes to amazement as she immediately recognizes Steven looking up and directly at her from down on one knee about 10 feet in front her. He appears just as surprised to see her, then he also takes notice of the room he's in. He's holding his hands to his stomach, and when he notices Vicky glance at his hands, he releases his stomach from his hands and looks down at them.

"Steven?"

"No blood...," He says with a stunned look on his face.

"What?... Blood?... What are you talking about?"

"Vicky, I'm not bleeding."

"Steven, what are you talking about? Why would you be bleeding?"

"I was just shot."

"What? Steven..."

"Yea..., I was shot in the stomach just a moment ago, and..."

"Steven..."

"And then again he was going to shoot me..."

"Steven!!"

"He was about to shoot me in the head!!"

"Steven, your still dreaming!!"

Steven stands up and stops for a moment wondering quietly what this all means. The possibilities run through his mind once again. What really just happened back there? Did I get killed? And if so, where am I now? Why is Vicky here? Is any of this real?

"Steven, you're dreaming," Vicky says.

"Dreaming?... But this all seems so real. I mean, look at this place. Look at you. It all looks so real."

"It is real, Honey. I mean, I'm real and this place is real."

"So, Vicky... where are we?"

"This is your home. We live here. You, me and the boys."

Steven looks around and doesn't recognize anything about the room he and Vicky are in. Nothing in the room is even remotely familiar.

"Vicky, we don't live here. This isn't our home."

"Steven, you just left here with the boys a minute ago. You told me to wait here in this room and tell you some things."

"I don't remember telling you that."

"Steven, you need to listen closely to everything I tell you. This is very important and I don't know how much time we have."

"What do you mean?"

"Just shut up and listen."

Steven stops and at first he's irritated by Vicky's harsh tone but he quickly regains his composure so he can focus on the urgency of what she wants to tell him.

"Steven, your construction job will call you back to work for a month or two but then they'll lay you off again.

"What? What do you mean?"

"Just stay quiet and listen."

"The job market is really bad where you are and it doesn't get much better for a while. But it's a blessing in disguise. Working out there as a skilled laborer isn't what you were meant to do. You have a much greater talent within you that you will soon discover. You will tell stories that people want to read. You can write! And you will write! That's what you wanted me to tell you. You will write this story. About what has happened to you."

"Vicky, I'm not a writer."

"Steven, you will be."

Vicky picks up a hardcover book from the coffee table and hands it to Steven. Taking it, he looks at the jacket and immediately sees his name below a title that sounds familiar to him... "The Dream Traveler."

"I wrote this?"

Vicky takes the book back from him. "You will write this. If you don't, all this..., none of it will come true. But don't even think about that, Steven, It already happened. She sets the book back down on the coffee table. You're a success. This was just your first book. But you must believe in yourself. You will write, Steven. You told me to tell you this. And you told me to tell you specifically for you to write as if you were Martin Eden."

"Martin Eden? Who is he?"

"I don't know. I thought you would. You're the one that told me to tell you that."

"I did?"

"Just a while ago, before you left the house. You told me not to be frightened but that you were going to be dream traveling here to this room at this specific time and to tell you all of this. You specifically said to make sure to tell you to write as if you were Martin Eden."

"Martin Eden?"

"Yes... you said it was very important that I tell you to remember that name, and remember this day... October 26, 2014, 8:00 pm."

"What's so important about that day and time?"

"That's today... October 26, 2014, now... it's 8 pm. Write it down when you wake up. Don't forget, Steven."

Steven repeats, "October 26, 2014, 8..." as he fades away waking up from his dream.

Chapter 52

2010
Saturday morning,
6:45 a.m.

Steven wakes up in bed and looks to his left where he sees Vicky is still sleeping. Sitting up feeling groggy, tired as if he had been awake and busy through the night, he tries to remember as much of the dream as he can. Working his way backwards through his memory he remembers talking to Vicky in what appeared to be a room in a very nice upscale house... "she said it was our house. It looked so nice. How could we ever afford such a place? She made it an important point that I remember the date and time, October, 26, 2014... 8 pm." He quickly sits up in bed, opens his night stand top drawer, pulls out a pencil and grabs whatever paper source he can find to write on. He doesn't find a note pad but instead he pulls out what appears to be the envelope of an old utility bill. Immediately he jots down the date and time: October 26, 2014, 8 pm, and "The Dream Traveler" under it. "Was it real?", He wonders to himself, "Hey, at least I'm alive... She said it was important that I remember this."

"Oh crap, the name of the guy? What was it?... Martin something... She told me I was supposed to write as if I were him, but I don't even know who he is. How am I supposed to do that if I don't even know who he is?" Steven writes the name Martin.

Getting out of bed he places the envelope and pencil down on the nightstand, stretching and yawning as he walks out of the bedroom and into the bathroom.

As he washes his face he remembers the gunfire and being shot in the gut. Then having the gun pointed to his forehead and thinks about how he managed not to get shot. It was supposed to happen that way. He'd seen it happen. "Thank God it's all over," He thinks, "Should I really write a book about everything that happened? Nobody would ever believe it... I would have to write it as a fiction story. That's the only way I could write it. Otherwise people would think I were crazy. Man, I must be crazy just to even believe it happened to me."

*

In the kitchen Vicky is preparing breakfast. Steven finishes telling Vicky what he can remember of his dream as she continues flipping pancakes on the griddle.

"So if this Martin person was so important, why

couldn't I remember his name when I woke up? Why would I tell you to give me the name of a writer who's name I didn't even remember?"

"Yea, it sounds like he's a famous writer or something the way you said I told you to write as if you were him. Still if he were so famous, you'd think we would have heard of him or something. You should check on the internet to see if you could come up with something."

"Vicky, I'm not even sure where to start."

"Steven, as much as you enjoy reading novels now and then, I can't believe you never heard of this writer. Maybe he doesn't even exist. Maybe you were just dreaming of something that isn't real."

"Vicky, if you would've seen this house we lived in, believe me, you would want it to be real."

Steven opens the laptop turns it on and waits for the home screen to load. As the computer boots up, he sits about the possibility that maybe the whole dream was just one that doesn't really mean anything more than ones where he would be flying through the sky like superman, or swimming under water and being able to breath fully submerged as if he had gills like a fish. Looking past the laptop and across the table he sees a book laying face down. An older looking book that appeared to have been checked out of a library. Getting up from his seat and moving to the book he wonders to himself if he really has what it takes to write a book. "I've never tried to write a book before," He thinks, "Something like this could take years to do." He turns the book over to see the front cover. Call of the Wild by Jack London.

"Call of the Wild. I've heard of this story. Is Erick reading this?"

"Yeah, I think he's reading it for a school book

report or something."

Steven opens the book to the front and there he finds a list of the many other books written by Jack London. Among them one titled, Martin Eden.

"Vicky!!!"

Vicky almost drops a pancake from the spatula as she's startled by Steven.

"Vicky, this is him!!"

"What? Really?"

"Martin Eden. That was the name of the writer I was supposed to remember. But Martin Eden isn't a writer. It's a title of another book written by Jack London. Where did this book come from?"

"I don't know. I think Erick checked it out of the school library."

Steven opened it up to the first chapter and began reading. Though he read many other novels, the words on the page drew his attention like nothing he ever read before. Putting the book down he decides immediately that he need to find the book titled Martin Eden by Jack London so he could read it.

"Steven, do you really think you can write a whole book? It's a lot of work you know."

"I know I can. I've already seen it. And I already know what the title is. But I think I need to read this book first."

"You can't copy something someone else wrote."

"I don't plan on copying it. But I sense there's something in this other story that might inspire me to succeed, I think I need to read it. I already know I can do this. Like I said, I've seen it. Vicky, we're gonna be doing better, a few years from now. I know it. And you're going to be there with me to share in our success."

"Steven, you're a success to me right now, just the way you are. You always have been. Always will be."

"Thank you, chocolate."

"De nada, peanut butter."

END

Acknowledgement

Special thanks to my brother Ben who without his encouragement this project may have never gotten off the ground. And to my friends and family who expressed confidence in me. And of course to Jesus Christ who with his help all things are possible.

Made in the USA
Middletown, DE
10 August 2016